TAKE ME FAST

BRIDGEWATER COUNTY - BOOK 3

VANESSA VALE

Cover design: Bridger Media

Cover graphic: Hot Damn Stock

GET A FREE BOOK!

JOIN MY MAILING LIST TO BE THE FIRST TO KNOW OF NEW
RELEASES, FREE BOOKS, SPECIAL PRICES AND OTHER
AUTHOR GIVEAWAYS.

http://freeromanceread.com

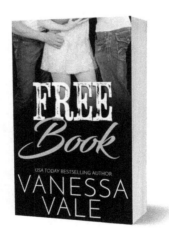

PROLOGUE

$\mathcal{I}$vy

Seven years ago

Even through the sleeping bag, the bed of Cooper's rusty old truck was hard beneath my back, but I didn't care. Not when I finally had what I wanted. *Who* I wanted—times two.

Rory was on top of me, his lean yet solid weight settling between my thighs so I could the feel thick outline of his hard cock. My skirt had slid up so my wet panties were pressed against his jeans.

My head was cradled on Cooper's arm and his breath whispered across my cheek as his free hand slipped inside my cotton button-down blouse. Deft fingers found my furled nipple through my lacy bra. I must have moaned because Rory stilled above me, his hips stopped grinding against me and he pulled away from the hot, wet, messy kiss that had started this whole business.

For a second, I thought maybe he was stopping because someone had heard my sound. But, no. We were parked out in the middle of Baker's field, far from town. The night was inky black, only the rising moon offering us light. There was no one around for miles, just the sound of a lone coyote in the distance a reminder of where we were.

It was Cooper who broke the silence, his deep voice gentle by my ear. "Are you sure, Ivy? We've just wanted you for so long. Too long. We don't have to do this if you don't want."

I bit back a groan of frustration, arched my back into his palm. My pussy was aching, throbbing, begging to be fucked. But I wasn't just horny for anyone—I wanted these boys. Both of them. I had for ages.

Cooper and Rory.

We'd grown up together, so I'd known them since forever, but our timing had never been right. By the time they took notice of me, I'd given up hope of them and had a boyfriend. Tom was nice and all, and I'd hoped that he might make me change my mind about Cooper and Rory. I'd watched from a distance as they grew up, filled out... became men. But it wasn't until graduation that I finally called it quits with Tom. I told him it was because I was leaving Bridgewater, off to college in Seattle. That was partly the reason, but I also ended it with him because one thing had become abundantly clear—Tom had never turned me on the way Rory and Cooper did with just a smoldering look across a crowded party or with an easy conversation at one of the high school bonfires. I'd fooled myself long enough. I hadn't had sex with him because I hadn't been ready. I might have been if Tom had been for me. But he wasn't.

I wanted Cooper and Rory and no one else would do. I felt things for them, things I hadn't even understood. At least until now.

My parents had left me with my grandmother when I was a baby and Grandma's idea of the sex talk was to show me some pictures of insects and flowers. None of those pictures prepared me for the firestorm that erupted inside me whenever Cooper and Rory were near. Some sort of electric current between us made my skin hot, my panties wet, and my stomach do flip flops.

I'd thought I'd known what attraction was, but I'd been clueless. Now, thanks to Rory and Cooper, I'd finally gotten a taste of what it meant to be desired and to be wanted, but our timing sucked yet again. If I'd just known they'd been interested sooner. If they'd told me. *If*...enough ifs. Summer was almost over, and once it ended, we'd all be going our separate ways.

Cooper and Rory were still frozen beside and above me, their hands frustratingly still as they waited for my answer. I'd heard some guys just took what they wanted, but not these two. The look of concern was sweet but I couldn't figure out why they'd stopped. This was what I'd wanted for so long—*they* were what I'd wanted—and now it was so close I could taste it, *feel* it. I shifted, trying to get closer to them.

"I'm sure," I breathed, wiggling my hips and making Rory hiss out a breath. I reached up, stroked his dark locks back, although they just fell over his forehead again. "I want my first time to be with you. With both of you."

To most, it would be crazy to be eighteen and want my first time to be with two guys. But this was Bridgewater. Two guys were the norm.

"We weren't thinking it would go this far," Rory said,

3

stroking a thumb over my cheek. Besides having my blouse open a few buttons, we were all still fully dressed. "That you'd want to, at least tonight. Shit, I didn't, um, we don't have any condoms."

"It's okay," I whispered, my cheeks growing hot under their watchful stares, and I hoped they couldn't see it in the moonlight. "I'm on the Pill." I didn't know why I was embarrassed. I wasn't the only girl in our school having sex, or in my case, going to. I'd gone to Dr. Murphy the day I'd turned eighteen. I'd already broken up with Tom, but I'd told myself I wanted to be ready when I got to college.

As I stared up at Rory's heavy-lidded gaze and heard Cooper's labored breathing beside me, I couldn't lie to myself any longer. I'd gone on the Pill because I'd hoped against hope that this would happen. I'd been dreaming about being fucked by these boys for months and now they were acting like they were too gentlemanly to give me what I needed. I loved that about them, but screw it.

Arching my hips up, I pressed my pussy against Rory's erection again. "I know what I'm doing. I want this."

I watched Rory's jaw clench, but he didn't move. He seemed to be waiting for Cooper's verdict.

I turned my head to look at Cooper, the fair-haired one —the sweet and gentle one. Not that Rory wasn't sweet...but he sure as hell wasn't gentle. I knew when they took me, they'd do it just like their personalities; Rory with wild abandon, Cooper with patience and deliberation.

Cooper tucked my hair behind my ear with the hand that had just been fondling my breasts. His pale gaze met mine, held. "God knows we want you so fucking bad, sweets. We always have. But we're going to be leaving soon..."

A whole new kind of ache swept over me. Sadness. Regret. Something close to nostalgia, even though that didn't make any sense at all. We all knew that this would be the one and only chance we had since I was leaving for college in a couple days and these boys had enlisted in the army. We were in a little bubble in the back of the pickup. Alone. Together. Safe.

This was it. Our one chance.

I forced a smile for Cooper's sake. "I know." I drew in a deep breath. "All the more reason for us to have this one night, don't you think?"

Cooper grinned and leaned in to give me a long, lingering kiss as Rory growled above me. He started grinding against me again and I spread my legs wider, giving him total access.

My words worked. All hesitation was gone and both boys sprang into action, fumbling with the remainder of the buttons on my shirt and the zipper of my skirt. Rory gave up on the skirt and tugged my panties off in one move. They raced to take off their own clothes and soon I was staring up at two very naked, very *hot* young men.

My mouth gaped when I caught sight of their cocks standing at attention as they hovered over me. Holy shit, they were big and they were ready. I'd seen pictures of them in magazines and online, but they weren't anything like this. Thick and long, hard too, both pointed right at me.

After that it was something of a blur. We were all hands and mouths as we greedily groped and kissed and licked and sucked.

Cooper took me first, settling between my parted thighs and nudging at my eager entrance. He swallowed the cry of pain as he carefully took my virginity. As he did so, Rory whispered in my ear telling me how beautiful I was, how perfect we were together, how he couldn't wait to have me. He reached between Cooper and I, found my clit with his thumb as Cooper continued to slowly move. To slide deep then pull almost all the way out. The combination was too much. I clawed at his back, pulling him deeper, wanting more. Faster. Wanting it all. I threw my head back and screamed up at the stars. After that, I lost track of how many times they made me come, how many times they took turns fucking me. Until the three of us were lost in each other, until there was nothing between us.

1

COOPER

Today

Seven years away and nothing had changed in Bridgewater. Rory sat across from me at one of the back booths in Jessie's diner, situated on Main Street, and the epicenter of life for the community. Gossip spread faster than butter on their hot pancakes. The booths were still red, the counters white with gold sparkle in them. The same jukebox stood in the corner as it had when we were kids. Hell, it even smelled the same—like coffee and grilled onions.

We'd come back to Bridgewater for visits over the years, but this time we were here to stay. No deployment loomed. No thoughts of months of desert sand and enemies we couldn't see. Because of this, I couldn't help but notice it all in a new light. Living in Bridgewater again felt surreal. But we weren't eighteen anymore, fresh out of high school with the girl of our dreams between us.

Across from me, Rory was slumped down in his seat with the same brooding expression he'd always worn. When Jessie approached our table with a welcoming smile, I watched him transform before my eyes. He sat up straight and took his hat off out of respect. Even gave the older woman a quick smile.

I pulled the sleeve of my long-sleeve T-shirt down to cover one of my scars. While everything was still the same, I'd changed. Some ways more obvious than others and not so much for the better.

"Well, I'll be damned." Jessie came to a stop beside our booth, a nearly full carafe of coffee in her hand. She wore the familiar lime green uniform. While her hair had a few more threads of gray, she looked good. She was like a warm ray of sunshine; someone who always had a quick smile, or a few moments for some juicy gossip. "I guess the rumors were right. The prodigal sons have returned."

Yup, lots of gossip. I just never imagined Rory or I would be the latest news.

I tried to return her smile but I'd lost the easy grin I used to be known for. I'd lost a lot of things during our tours of Afghanistan. When we enlisted in the fall after graduation, we both trained to become helicopter pilots. After years training and working stateside, we'd been shipped overseas. To war. The first tour went fine. Well, as fine as a tour in the Middle East could go. But this last trip had taken me as close to hell as I was willing to go.

Rory and I had agreed that our days in the military were over. After my accident, the powers-that-be agreed I'd served my time and we'd both been honorably discharged. Now, we were back in our hometown and ready to make a new start, but adjusting to our old lives was harder than I'd anticipated. Part of the reason we were here at the diner was to escape my family.

God love 'em, they were only trying to help. But my parents and my younger sisters didn't know the first thing about what I'd been through. They only knew that I'd come back scarred and distant. They were just happy I was whole —or almost whole—and home. Their attempts to help me adjust back to life in Bridgewater left me feeling more like an outsider. A charity case. The more they catered to me, the more I itched to run back to the military. At least there I knew where I belonged.

Rory understood better than anyone. He always had. While he hadn't been shot out of the sky, he could relate.

Jessie filled up the empty coffee mug in front of me. "On the house for our returning heroes."

I tried not to wince at those words, but I saw Rory grimace on my behalf. We'd left visiting with my smothering family to avoid that kind of talk. I might not know who I was these days, but I knew who I wasn't. I wasn't the hero everyone was making me out to be.

We'd always been protective of each other—Rory was the closest thing to a brother I'd ever had. But ever since the crash, he seemed to think it was his personal mission to keep me from any uncomfortableness whatsoever. His intentions were good, but what he and my family couldn't seem to understand was that no amount of coddling would make the pain go away. My wounds had healed to ugly scars, but the wounds to my mind, to my psyche, I doubted would ever fade.

During this last tour, my helicopter went down during a routine mission. I was the pilot transporting six soldiers. Anti-aircraft fire had hit the tail and I'd fought to keep us airborne, but it had been a fucking lost cause. I'd been injured, put in the hospital for months, but I was the lucky one. I was the one who survived. The only one. I should be grateful, but it was hard to feel lucky when all I could think about was the men who hadn't made it. Who I'd killed because I hadn't kept the chopper in the sky. Why did I get to go home when they didn't?

I saw Jessie's gaze flicker down to the scar that was peeking beneath my sleeve. "You doing okay, hon?" Her smile slipped a little as if she sensed my mood.

Her intentions were good, I had no doubt about that. But I couldn't bring myself to respond. What could I say? Was I doing okay? No. But no one wanted to hear that answer. No one wanted to know the war hero was fucked up.

"So, what's new in town, Jessie?" Rory changed the topic to avoid any further awkward silences. Funny, that used to be my role. I'd been the chatty one. The easygoing one. The one who could make conversation with anyone at any time. To smooth things over when Rory's family life had been shit. Now *he* was the one who had to keep the conversation going when it grew too uncomfortable or someone asked the wrong question.

I didn't mind the silence, but I knew it drove Rory nuts.

"There's got to be some better gossip than us two returning." His tone was too bright, too cheerful, as he tried to steer the conversation away from me, away from us. Away from what we'd been through overseas.

"Well, let's see now," Jessie started. "I suppose you heard that the Kane boys found themselves a wife."

Rory nodded. "We met Katie during our last trip home. Sweet girl." We'd been a year behind Sam Kane in school. His cousin, Jack, was a little bit older.

"Did you hear we have a new doctor?" She looked at me with raised brows, like she was waiting for me to comment.

"Is that right?" I mumbled, not surprised Dr. Murphy retired. He'd been around since I was a kid. He'd even set my broken arm when I was six. I'd jumped out of the big cottonwood in the back yard thinking I was Superman. I wasn't then and I wasn't now. It seemed I didn't do a good job of staying in the air. That time, it had only been me who'd gotten hurt.

"Yes, sir. Hannah worked here at the diner for a while before taking up with Cole and Declan. You remember those boys, don't you?"

"Yes, ma'am."

Rory was toying with his coffee mug and I knew exactly what was coming.

"Any news on Ivy Walters?"

There it was. *Ivy.* The one who'd gotten away. We'd had our eyes on her for years back in high school. For the last few weeks of the summer, we'd done everything together—including one wild night of fucking—and we decided a long time ago that was how we liked it. My parents had a Bridgewater marriage—two men sharing one wife—and Rory and I vowed back then we'd do the same. With Ivy Walters.

It had been no secret we both wanted her and it was no secret—at least now that Rory asked Jessie about her— we wanted her still. In Bridgewater, both of us interested in her was perfectly normal.

And Bridgewater men? We knew how to find our

woman. Call it fate or just a gut instinct, but when Bridgewater men found their mate, they just knew. And that's how it was for Rory and me. After that night with Ivy, when she gave us the precious gift of her virginity, she became ours. She was the one, but she'd slipped through our fucking fingers.

With that long blonde hair and perfect curves, we hadn't been the only guys with out-of-control hormones after Ivy back then. No, she'd had a boyfriend for most of senior year. Fuck, Tom something. It hadn't been serious, but it had been hard to see them together out on dates. They'd broken up, and finally we'd had our one night.

Only one fucking night.

But it had been perfect. Ivy had admitted she wanted us as much as we'd wanted her. And Tom? Well, we learned firsthand that he never claimed her. She'd been a virgin that night. She might have dated Tom, but she'd given herself to us. My cock had been her first. I grew hard just remembering how she'd felt, how her eyes had widened in the moonlight when I took her deep, stretched her open. Filled her up with my cum. Then it had been Rory's turn and she'd eagerly taken him, too.

That one time was enough for us to know, even all these years later...she was the one. We'd only been eighteen, wet-behind-the-ears boys and yet we hadn't forgotten her. I thought of her often, wondered what she'd done with her life after her grandmother had passed away. All we knew was that after the funeral she'd never come back to Bridgewater. If she had, we would have known. If she had, we would have gone out to Baker's field and had her all over again. This time, we wouldn't come within two minutes. We'd seen to her pleasure, but now? Now, we'd take care of her like two men could. Not just in the bedroom, but in life. We'd protect her, love her, cherish her. Make her ours in every way. Put a fucking ring on her finger.

Of course, we couldn't do jack shit about it at the time. Not with her going off to college in Seattle to become a teacher and us heading into the army. We'd never hold her back from her dreams and on top of that, we'd had nothing to offer her. She'd had to go and we'd let her. And since she was ours, we couldn't hold her back. We had to give her everything that she needed, that she deserved, and that included leaving us for school. And so she'd gone west and we'd gone east to boot camp and then to the Middle East to war.

But now...well, now we'd saved up some money. Being deployed to a sandbox didn't give much opportunity to spend any of it. We had enough to open our own helicopter business for tourists and the like. With the Rocky Mountains and Yellowstone National Park nearby, scenic tours were popular. Same went for taking well-off hunters and campers into the backcountry. Well, Rory would take them and I'd push papers. Regardless, we were back for good, with a solid plan for our business and more than ready to move on from the military.

All we were missing was our woman.

We aimed to get her back...if we could find her. We'd been trying to track her down for seven years, ever since we said goodbye to her and went our separate ways. At first we'd sent letters to her grandmother's house from boot camp, but each and every one was returned. We found out later that her grandmother had passed away that first fall and her house was sold. Then we tried to track her down at that college she'd headed off to in Seattle, but found out she'd only been enrolled for one semester. Then nothing.

The woman we planned to marry had fallen off the face of the earth.

Every time we returned to Bridgewater for a family visit we always asked around, but no one seemed to know what became of Ivy. Word must have spread, because Jessie was giving Rory a knowing smile.

"You two still hung up on that girl?" She looked up and waved to someone who'd come through the front door. "It's been years now since she left this town behind."

Jessie turned to me and I did my best impersonation of the old Cooper—the one without the scars and the nightmares. I gave her my best slow, lazy smile. "Yes, ma'am. We've had our heart set on Ivy for a long time now. We just can't seem to track her down."

Something shifted in Jessie's expression. Some of the teasing faded and she seemed to be studying me closely. Too closely. But whatever she saw seemed to make an impression. "You know, I don't normally gossip—"

I ignored the smirk Rory shot my way from behind her back. Everyone knew Jessie had all the news in town and wasn't afraid to share it. But apparently she had a code of ethics when it came to gossip.

"Normally I wouldn't share that girl's business with anybody, but I know you boys and I do believe you're only asking because you care about Ivy."

I shot Rory a quick look and saw the same shock in his eyes. Was this it? Had we finally gotten a lead on our lady?

"That's the truth," Rory said, holding up his fingers like he was still a Boy Scout. "That girl stole our hearts back when we were kids, and we aim to make her ours."

Rory might have been laying it on thick, but he was telling the truth and Jessie must have seen that because her gaze softened until she looked downright emotional. "That's what I was hoping you would say."

I gripped my mug tight to keep from showing my impatience, but God almighty, we'd been waiting seven years to find Ivy. "Do you know where she is, Jessie?"

She drew in a deep breath. "I sure do." She paused and I thought for sure I'd have to sweet talk it out of her, but then she said in a rush, "She's in Seattle."

I hadn't realized just how hopeful I'd become until those hopes came crashing down. I saw Rory's shoulders sag as well. He still mustered a small smile. "We tried Seattle. She said she was going to school there, but she only registered for one semester. We couldn't track her down after that."

He looked my way and it didn't take a psychic to read his mind. *Another dead end.*

Jessie made a sound of disgust that had us looking up at her once more.

"My goodness, for two grown men who've seen something of the world, you sure are dense."

I stared up at her in surprise. "Excuse me?"

"If you'd asked the right questions all these years, you would have gotten the answer straight away."

Rory leaned forward over the table and I could tell he was fighting the same battle to avoid losing patience with the older woman. "And what questions would that be?"

Jessie talked slowly as if to two morons. "After her grandmother passed, what other family did she have left?"

Rory and I shared a blank look, one that said *who the hell knows*?

Everyone knew that Ivy's parents split when she was a baby. Her mama was young when she got knocked up and she and Ivy's dad didn't want the burden. They hadn't wanted to be trapped in Bridgewater, from what I heard. So they dropped Ivy off at her grandma's and never came back. I remembered hearing that story for the first time when I was a kid and wondered how in hell Ivy could be so sweet and trusting with parents like that. Her grandmother must have done something right to keep her from feeling bitter and abandoned.

Rory was the first to answer. "Her parents, I suppose. But I thought she didn't have anything to do with them."

Jessie sighed and glanced over as the chimes above the door signaled another new customer. The mealtime rush was coming in. "She doesn't. No one's heard from her mother and that fool boyfriend of hers in years. They didn't even show up for her grandmother's funeral." Jessie scowled at the thought. "Probably too ashamed to show their faces."

I saw the customers take a seat and knew we were running out of time before Jessie had to get back to work. "She didn't have any other family, did she?"

"Not immediate family, no," Jessie said. The way she stressed *immediate* made it instantly clear. I sat up straight and tried not to get my hopes up too much. Who knew how accurate town gossip was? And that's what this was. Rumors. Yet I wanted to reach out and shake Jessie to get her to spit it out. She was enjoying this way too much.

"She has a great aunt," Jessie said. "Her grandmother's sister. In Seattle."

For the first time in what felt like forever, some of the weight I'd been carrying slipped away. We might have returned to town and started a business, started to put down some roots. But they would mean nothing without Ivy.

After a million dead ends, we finally had a lead. We had fucking hope and I hadn't had that in a long, long time.

Rory gave me a shit-eating grin, stood and kissed Jessie on the cheek. The woman smiled and preened at the surprising burst of affection. "Jessie, if we didn't have our hearts set on Ivy, you'd be the one for us."

Jessie sputtered, then patted him on the shoulder before going off to fill more coffee cups down the line of booths.

I stood, tossed a few bills on the table, then looked to Rory. Yeah, he was right there with me. I could see the eagerness, the hope, in his eyes. "Let's go get our girl."

2

$\mathcal{I}$VY

Even though school was over for the year, the kids off enjoying the start to their summer break, my last teacher work day had been jam-packed with faculty meetings and cleaning out my classroom. I had an hour before I had to pick up Lily from her summer camp. Enough time for me to get some groceries so I could make dinner for me, Lily, and my great aunt, Sarah. The sky was clear for once and I hoped to eat outside on the patio.

I loaded up the last box of classroom supplies and carried it to the parking lot. One of my coworkers called out, "Have a great summer, Ivy!"

Smiling, I turned to reply but stopped so suddenly my mouth was left hanging open.

If my coworker noticed, she didn't say anything. Or, if she did, I didn't hear her. I was far too focused on the two men who were blocking the path to my car. I swear my heart skipped a beat, then took off like a runaway train at the sight of them. They were leaning against a red sedan like they belonged there in the parking lot of this Seattle suburb elementary school.

Cooper and Rory.

But they didn't belong there. They didn't belong *here*, in my world. My home.

Oh god. My head started spinning and that was when I realized that I'd stopped breathing. I inhaled deeply, hoping a little oxygen would make some sort of sense out of what I was seeing. *Who* I was seeing.

It couldn't be them.

But it was. There was no doubt. I would recognize Cooper and Rory anywhere. Even here, now, and looking like they did. They weren't boys anymore. That was my first thought as my gaze greedily drank in the sight of them. They shouldn't be here. I didn't want them here.

Yes, I did.

No, I didn't. I couldn't.

Yet somehow the sight of them was a relief. Like getting a sip of water after being so dang thirsty it hurt to swallow.

They'd survived the military, come home. *Come here.*

With no more connections to Bridgewater after my grandmother died and I settled permanently in Seattle, I hadn't heard what had happened to them. It hadn't stopped me from wondering, to check the Bridgewater newspaper online and ensure there wasn't an obituary for either of them. God, tears threatened at the thought, then at the sight of them.

I didn't know how long I stood there staring. Long enough for them to take a good long look at me in return.

"It's been a long time, Ivy." *That voice.* It had said dirty words to me that night. The one night we shared. Perfect

19

words. Rory was the first to break the silence between us. God, he was still hot as hell. He'd always been good looking —the epitome of tall, dark, and handsome. But now...well, now he could add brawny, muscular, and chiseled to that description. He looked taller, heavier, packed with muscle. His dark hair was cut shorter than it had been in high school; it no longer fell over his forehead. But then, I supposed that was a side effect of his military lifestyle. He wore a snug black T-shirt and faded jeans, and he filled out the shirt to perfection. Even from where I stood a couple of yards away I could see the biceps bulging beneath the short-sleeves.

Rory took a step toward me, but Cooper stayed where he was leaning against the car. He looked the same...but different, if that made any sense. He still had the same blond hair and boyish good looks, but there was something guarded about him now. Wary. His blue eyes weren't filled with laughter like I remembered and that easy smile was nowhere to be seen. He tipped his head when my gaze met his and for a moment I had the crazy urge to run to him and hold him tight. To feel his beating heart, to feel his breathing, his strong grip. To know he would never let go.

They were both still watching me. Still staring. I realized that I still hadn't said a word. They were waiting for me to speak.

Problem was, I had no idea what to say. I wasn't even sure how I felt at seeing them. No, I knew. Stunned obviously speechless. Scared, which was a given. I'd never planned on seeing these two ever again. I'd prayed they would go home to Bridgewater alive, but I never expected them to come here, to find me. Not after that night when my life got turned upside down. Now that the shock of seeing them was starting to pass, the significance of their visit hit me hard and nerves made my stomach churn.

Oh god. Did they learn about Lily? Was that why they'd come? To take her away? There was only one way to find out.

"What...what are you doing here?" The words came out through stiff lips and my tone was colder than I'd intended. Rory's head jerked back as if I'd slapped him, but Cooper didn't flinch at the harsh greeting. He just kept staring at me with those pale blue eyes. Eyes I saw in my dreams. Something about the way he was looking at me made me cross my arms in front of my chest as if I could physically shield him from looking too closely and seeing too much. Of discovering the truth. Yes, I'd changed, too. I was no longer eighteen. I'd had a child. My breasts weren't what they used to be and I had more curves, broader hips. And while they couldn't see them through my clothes, stretch marks.

Rory recovered quickly and his lips curved up into that lopsided grin that used to make my knees weak. The way they felt rubbery now meant he still could. I drew in an unsteady breath.

"You're a hard woman to track down," he said.

My spine stiffened at that. So they'd been looking for me for a while then. *Shit.* I shrugged. "It's not like I was hiding." That was the truth. I hadn't taken any drastic measures to hide from Rory and Cooper...but I hadn't gone out of my way to seek them out, either.

I left a lot behind when I moved from Bridgewater. When Grandma died first semester freshman year, I had no reason to go back. I'd been reeling from grief and only a month or so into college classes...that was when I'd learned I was pregnant. Eighteen and pregnant, just like my mother. But unlike her, I hadn't had Grandma to turn to. Instead of the dorms, I'd stayed with Grandma's sister, Aunt Sarah, to save money, but we both agreed that schooling would have to wait until I had the baby and it was older.

I'd ached to call them, to tell them they were going to have a child, but I couldn't. They'd wanted to serve their country and I knew they would have walked away if they had a responsibility elsewhere. Besides, it had been my fault I'd gotten pregnant. I'd been the one to tell them condoms weren't necessary. I had been on the Pill. It hadn't been a lie. I just hadn't known about the issue with antibiotics weakening the effectiveness. My stupidity hadn't been their fault. While Lily was far from a burden, neither of them had wanted a child right out of high school. At first, I'd thought they'd reach out to me, but time marched on and they never did, so I never contacted them.

It may have taken a little longer, but I still managed to get my degree in education and the job of my dreams teaching at an elementary school. It had taken years, but I'd finally gotten my life together after the unexpected pregnancy nearly derailed me.

And now that I had it all worked out—a good life, a beautiful daughter, a great job—these two had to show up and throw my life for a loop all over again. Just seeing them stirred up all kinds of feelings I'd buried. Deep. I forced myself to ask the question I feared the most. "Why were you looking for me?"

Cooper finally spoke then, his gaze never faltering. "We think you know the answer to that, Ivy."

My heart stopped in my chest. What the hell did that mean? They somehow learned about Lily and wanted her?

He took another step and he was close enough that I could see his eyes. Really see them. The hurt, the darkness. My heart ached for what I remembered seeing, for what was missing now. He'd always been so happy, so carefree. I hated to think what had happened to make those blue eyes so hard.

Rory moved toward me then too, and it took everything in me not to back away. I knew they wouldn't hurt me, but they could ruin everything I'd created for me and Lily, whether they meant to or not.

"We came for you, Ivy," Rory said.

I stopped breathing as his words registered. Looking from him to Cooper and back again, I thought for one second maybe they were joking. They couldn't be serious. What came out of my mouth was somewhere between a laugh and a gasp. It ended up sounding like I was choking on air.

Rory was still wearing that sexy grin, but Cooper was most certainly not laughing. "We've missed you, Ivy. We want you in our life."

I shook my head to clear it, because honestly, Cooper's words were affecting me far more than I wanted to admit. A warmth spread through me because of what he'd said as well as their almost tender looks. Stares that said better than words that they really *had* missed me. That they wanted me in their lives.

Oh god, *they wanted me in their lives.*

That heat spread down to my core as I caught their looks of desire. I squeezed my thighs together to ease the ache. Oh hell, they wanted *me.* And I still did, it seemed. I never stopped.

I shook my head slightly, trying to organize my thoughts. It didn't matter that they wanted me. I wasn't a teenage girl anymore. I was an adult, with responsibilities. And, most importantly, a child. With that thought in mind, I forced myself to walk past them to my car using the box as a damn shield.

"What we had is ancient history," I said as I passed. "It was one night. It didn't mean anything."

"That sounds like a challenge," Rory called after me.

I felt a smile tugging at my lips at his teasing tone. Goddammit, he was still charming as hell. I didn't trust myself to turn around, too afraid they'd see the same desire mirrored in my eyes, or the smile that wanted to spread at the thought of them spending so much time and energy finding me. It felt good to know they'd thought of me, too. That I hadn't just been one night to them, regardless of what I was saying. It hadn't been just one night for me. Not just because of Lily as a living reminder of our time together, but because I hadn't had anyone since. Not like them.

"It's not a challenge," I said as I popped the trunk with my key fob and put the box inside. Going around the car, I opened the driver's door, then turned to face them. "I've moved on. It's time you guys do, too."

The words felt like shards of glass coming out of my throat, but I'd forced them out anyway. Yeah, in my dream world I would have loved to go back to whatever motel they were staying at and fuck them silly. No, to grab hold of them and never let go. But it wasn't about me and what I wanted. I had a daughter to think about. Lily deserved to have a solid home life, which was what she had with me and Aunt Sarah. I'd made my decision to leave these guys in the past and it was no use second guessing that choice now. No matter how ruggedly handsome they were. They couldn't just be hot cowboys. No, they had to be brash military men, too. That combination was lethal to my defenses and made my ovaries jump for joy.

Women everywhere deserved to hate me for refusing them.

Cooper's low, hard voice made me pause before I could slide into the driver's seat. "You can't get rid of us that easily, Ivy. You're ours—you always have been."

I couldn't respond. My heart had jumped up into my throat, making speech impossible. *You're ours*. He couldn't be saying what I thought he was saying, right? Spinning around to face him, I was dumbstruck by the intensity of his gaze. Rory's posture was more relaxed, but those dark eyes of his were fixed on me like I was his key to salvation. It scared me if he thought I was.

"You don't mean that." It was the first thing I could think to say and even to my own ears it sounded like another challenge. But that wasn't what I meant. I meant...ah hell, I didn't know what I meant.

Rory moved forward so he was standing beside Cooper. "We want you back, Ivy. We want you in our life."

"Just like that? After seven years? I might be married."

"Are you?" Cooper asked, his gaze lowering to my left hand.

I couldn't lie to them about that. There was no ring, no obvious proof I belonged to someone else. I shook my head.

"We've known all this time you're the one for us. We aim to prove it to you, if you'll let us."

"Just like that?" I shook my head frantically, unable to come up with the right words to make them understand. They weren't supposed to be here. They were no longer a part of my life. "Where have you been all this time?"

Cooper's eyes shuttered and Rory's jaw tightened. "War."

Rory's one word said it all, answered so many questions for me. War. These two had seen battle and survived, but they were changed by it. I knew them well enough, even after seven years, to know they weren't the same. Some of the anger left me then. They had been fighting to keep me and Lily safe. I couldn't complain about them staying away.

Occasionally, I'd thought about the possibility of running into them again and how I would handle it, but I never got far with that line of thinking because it seemed impossible. Especially now that I knew they were in some far-off desert fighting. It had been a hopeful daydream that I might one day see my high school crushes again, nothing more. In my daydreams, it was always *one day*. I never thought that day would come because I had no reason to go back to Bridgewater, not with Grandma gone. There hadn't been anything there for me there after that, not even them. Never in my wildest dreams had I imagined that they'd track me down. And that when they did, they'd stand before me and lay claim.

I might have moved away from Bridgewater seven years ago, but I'd been born and raised there, and I knew the town's customs. When Bridgewater men claimed a woman, they meant it for life. When they took me in the truck bed that hot summer night, they'd made me theirs. Even after all the time that had passed, to them, I still was theirs.

If I took a moment to admit it, I still wanted to be.

Panic made breathing difficult. I had a feeling my every thought and fear was written on my face and I did my best to keep it under control. Placing one hand on top of the car, I took a deep breath. "I'm not looking for a relationship. I don't want you to prove anything to me." They continued to stare, but they didn't interrupt. "I said it before and I'll say it again. I've moved on, and I think you should, too."

Cooper broke the staring contest first. He dropped his gaze and lifted a hand to scrub it across his face. He looked exhausted and worn out.

Some of the anger seeped out of my tone. "Look, I'm sorry you came all this way—"

Rory's jaw clenched as he glanced from me to Cooper and back again. "Just one dinner." His tone was firm, harsh almost, but his eyes were practically pleading.

I had no idea what was going on with these guys, but I couldn't bring myself to say no. Not right away, at least. Somehow it would have seemed cruel. How could one dinner hurt?

Rory must have sensed my hesitation because he crossed the distance between us in a few quick strides, stopping when he was right in front of me, blocking me in between his hard body, the car door and the car itself. So close I could smell his aftershave. He tilted his head down so he could speak softly. "Look, Ivy. You know as well as I do that we won't give up so easily. If there's no man in the way, no ring on that finger, then there's still a chance."

I glanced up at him and wished I hadn't. His slow smile was still sexy as hell and it made my belly clench as I remembered in vivid detail exactly what those lips felt like against mine. On my neck, my nipples, my inner thighs. He reached a hand out and brushed the back of his fingers along my cheek, as if I was something precious that he'd just discovered. Or someone he'd lost who'd now been found. My eyes fell closed at the tender caress. "Please, give us one night to show you just how good it could be."

Oh, my fucking stars. His low, sexy voice alone would have been enough to make me swoon. But add in that smoldering gaze and the hint of a promise that they'd rock my world—needless to say, my panties were wet. All he had to do was talk, for Cooper to give me a heated stare and I was more aroused than I'd been in years. My breath came in short pants as my brain processed his words and tried to come up with a reasonable response. By that I meant a response in which I didn't launch myself at him and beg him to fuck me right then and there.

I was telling them no and with just a few words I was a panty melting mess.

Focus, Ivy. I couldn't have them. These men were strictly off limits. I had to think of my family. My daughter.

But Rory's dark gaze never wavered, and while I couldn't see Cooper, I could *feel* his eyes on me as well.

That was when it truly hit me. They wouldn't give up. Not now, not ever—not unless I gave them a chance.

A hysterical laugh bubbled up in my chest, but I managed to swallow it down. What the fuck was I supposed to do? If I said no, they wouldn't stop until they'd changed my mind. Maybe even show up at my home. Not maybe, definitely.

"Are you all right?" Cooper asked. He'd come to join us and his eyes were crinkled up at the corners in concern. "You look awfully pale."

I nodded quickly. Yeah, I was fine. *Great.* I licked my lips and both of them stared at my mouth. "You have to admit you too are a little overwhelming."

They both grinned and it was possible I might have just come from that alone. Sweet baby Jesus, they were gorgeous. One fair, the other dark, but both...wow. I felt so small beside them, so feminine. They were bigger than I ever remembered. And their muscles? God handed out a few extra for these two.

I could either give these guys what they wanted and try my damnedest to get them to accept the fact that I'd moved on—okay, not really at all—or I could live in fear that they would show up unannounced on my doorstep.

My sigh was far from gracious. "All right, fine. One dinner."

They glanced at each other and at me like I'd just found the cure for cancer.

"That lacked the eagerness I was hoping for, but I'll take it," Rory said. He leaned in closer. "I'll take you, any way I can get you."

I imagined him taking me bent over the hood of my car, up against a wall, from behind...all kinds of dirty possibilities made me practically whimper.

We agreed on a time the following night—that would give me the opportunity to get my head on straight. Hopefully. I got Rory's phone number and promised to text them my address.

Cooper just shook his head and his gaze dropped to my lips. Instinctively, I licked them and I heard a rumble from deep in his chest. "It took us seven years to find you. We'll call you." He pulled out a cell from his shirt pocket and typed in the digits I gave him. Only then were they reassured and stepped back.

Before I could question my sanity or start hyperventilating, I said my goodbyes and slipped into my car.

It wasn't until I was standing there in the foyer of my aunt's house that I realized I'd never stopped at the store for groceries. I'd driven home in a trance, not even remembering parking the car in the driveway. Soon, I'd have to go and pick up Lily and I needed to pull myself together beforehand.

She was only six, but she was a perceptive little girl. I didn't want her asking questions about why I was acting funny. Why I wanted to reach down between my legs and touch myself, to make myself come. Because honestly, what could I say? *I'm freaking out because I saw your daddies today, sweetheart, and they were too hot to resist.*

I was so not ready to have that conversation, or at least a G-rated version of it.

I stared at my reflection in the entryway mirror. To their eyes, I probably looked the same as they remembered, or similar at least. I touched my shorter hair, saw that my makeup was more subdued. But I was still tall and slender, with the same heart-shaped face and blue eyes. I needed to make it clear to them that I might look the same, but looks could be deceiving. I wasn't that girl anymore and beneath my clothes, I wasn't nubile or eighteen. Were they interested in what we had together seven years ago or the woman I'd become? They said they wanted to learn more, but I'd shut them down, hadn't given them the chance. No, their chance was tomorrow night. One night.

You're ours—you always have been.

My heart fluttered in my chest at the thought. Back when I was a kid I used to think the Bridgewater way was romantic. Sweet, even. Two men sweeping me off my feet. I met my gaze in the mirror again. Now the Bridgewater way just scared the crap out of me. They thought I was the one. The. One. That I could be their future. My chest tightened painfully. There was no way, not after all this time and not with all the secrets between us. They might want me in their lives, but I didn't want them.

No, I did want them. Too much, and that was the problem. It wasn't just about me anymore.

The ache between my thighs that hadn't subsided called me a liar. I couldn't deny that I was still attracted to them, but I was a grown up now. I knew that attraction wasn't everything. It didn't necessarily equal commitment and family, and that was what I needed. Lily needed it. Deserved it.

I smirked at my reflection in the mirror. I supposed family was what they'd given me, in a roundabout way. Without them, without that one night, there would be no Lily, and she was my family. She was my everything. I'd given her a stable home and I wasn't about to let two near-strangers into her life to wreak havoc because they were hung up on one night seven years ago.

Besides, there was no telling what they'd do if they found out they had a child they knew nothing about.

3

It took Cooper way too long to open the door to his hotel room. I had to seek him out when he never showed up for breakfast and when he opened the door, I saw why. "You look like shit."

Cooper grimaced and winced at the light coming from the hallway. He headed back into the room, leaving me to follow, rubbing the back of his neck as he went.

"Did you get any sleep last night?" Shit. I hated when my tone took on that mother hen sound. It wasn't me. Or at least it hadn't been until nearly a year ago when Cooper stopped eating and sleeping unless someone forced him to. PTSD was a bitch. A ruthless bitch. He'd gotten better at day-to-day survival these past few months, therapy had helped, but I still found myself checking up on him, making sure he was getting by.

Not that my forcing him to eat a healthy meal now and

again made up for the fact that I'd ruined his life, but for now it was the best I could do. It had been my dream to go into the army, not his. I'd wanted out of my fucked up house and while he'd had a Leave It To Beaver family, he'd enlisted with me. Only to get blown out of the damn sky.

And now he wasn't sleeping because of nightmares. Haunted by the ghosts of those who'd died. Learning of Ivy's whereabouts had helped, but seeing her had fucked with him. I wasn't sure if it was because she hadn't leaped into either of our arms or her telling us we were seven years too late. Either way, reality was also a bitch.

Maybe it was because she was so fucking perfect, that he wanted her when those six soldiers who died would never know the feel of a woman's arms around his neck, the tight heat of her pussy.

When Cooper ignored my question and started digging through his backpack for a change of clothes, I knew I had my answer. He hadn't slept—at least not after the nightmare I was sure he'd had. I knew he had them about the crash more nights than not, how he wouldn't be able to sleep after. Sometimes he talked to me about them, but most often he kept quiet like he was doing now.

"Did you already eat?" he asked, heading toward the bathroom sink with a toothbrush in hand.

"Yeah, but I'll go back to the diner with you. I could use another cup of coffee."

Cooper's response was a snort of disbelief as he scratched his dick through his boxers. "You just want to make sure I eat breakfast."

I shrugged when he caught my eye in the mirror's reflection. Guilty. But his eyes? Bloodshot and full of guilt. Pain. Shame.

He shook his head before spitting out some toothpaste.

33

"I don't need you looking over my shoulder all the time. I've been eating three meals a day, like a good little boy."

I ignored his harsh, sarcastic tone. It was going to be one of those days. I just hoped he shook off the nightmare and the hangover that came with it before we picked Ivy up for our date.

"I could use another cup of coffee," I said. It was the truth, whether he believed me or not. I'd been up half the night too, though not with nightmares. I'd been thinking about Ivy...and how the fuck I was going to make sure she came back to Bridgewater with us. She was everything I remembered, and more. She'd been barely a woman then, all lean, sweet curves. Now? Now she was *all* woman. Lush breasts, rounded hips. Her hair was a touch darker, shorter, but it looked as silky as I when I'd run my fingers through it before. I wanted to touch her, discover every inch of her all over again. We were all different, changed, and so while we had a past together, we had to start over.

I was excited for that. Eager to discover the older, wiser Ivy. I just had to hope she wanted to do the same for us. We weren't the men who she remembered and it was going to be damn hard to get her to want two damaged souls. Just seeing the results of Cooper's rough night had me worried.

Everything was riding on this. I'd been dreaming about settling down with Ivy since forever. Fuck, since we took her home that night after we claimed her. Since we got on that bus to boot camp. Since we boarded the C-5 and headed to Afghanistan for the first tour. Then the second.

I knew it was the same for Cooper, although it would be harder for him to show it, to express his interest, his *hope*, and that was why it fell on me to make sure we won her over. Cooper needed her. I needed her, too, but Cooper... hell, he needed something positive in his life. Someone to love and take care of. To see that there was good in the world. Someone who would help him laugh again. That it was *okay* to laugh again.

I owed him this. Growing up with a deadbeat dad and an alcoholic mom, it was no wonder that I'd wanted to escape Bridgewater. All through high school, I couldn't wait to get out of my shitty house and Cooper had promised to stay by my side. We'd long since agreed that we'd find a woman together, and Cooper had taken it a step further by enlisting with me even though he had a damn near Norman Rockwell family.

It shouldn't have ended the way it did. Hearing my best friend had been shot down, that his chopper had crashed in the rugged fucking desert and they weren't sure if there were any survivors. Rushing to the field hospital to learn the truth, that he'd been the only one to survive, and barely. To be stuck in hell as he was shipped to Germany to recover. To have to finish out the last month of my damn tour before I could join him in DC at the rehab hospital. He was a "brother from another mother."

If anyone should have suffered physical and emotional pain, it should have been me. I'd always been the tough one, the strong one. Not that Cooper wasn't, fuck, he was the strongest man I knew, but he'd never had any need to be. He had a good life, grew up in a kind household. An amazing mother and two dads I respected the hell out of. Me...I'd been training my whole life to deal with pain and fight back against despair. I was used to it, being dealt the worst hands in a deck and dealing with it. Going all in even when the odds were against me. I could go to hell and come back laughing. Cooper...he was too good for that shit. He'd gone to hell, that was for damn sure, I just wasn't sure if he'd ever come back.

I followed him out of the hotel and across the street to the diner. His shattered leg had healed and I no longer had to slow my pace to match his. But the scars would remain. Obvious reminders to him—and anyone who saw his bare arms and torso, his left leg—of what had happened. I guessed that was how life worked—the people who got hurt weren't always the ones who deserved it. Life wasn't fair, I knew that. But it still sucked. And I still intended to do everything in my power to make things right and to give Cooper the kind of life he deserved.

That meant winning Ivy back and bringing her home with us so we could start a new life. Together. We'd only had one night to show her what she meant to us and we wanted a lifetime more.

Cooper remained too quiet until the coffee was poured and his eggs were set in front of him. He toyed with his food and I sat there patiently sipping from my mug. I knew he was deep in thought and he'd talk when he was ready. That still didn't prepare me for what he said.

"I think we should go back to Bridgewater." His bloodshot eyes met mine. "Today. This afternoon."

Setting my mug down, I tried to make sense of his request. "You mean, before we meet Ivy for dinner?"

He gave me a short nod.

"But we just found her." Leaning over the table, I tried not to let my frustration show. "After all these years, Cooper, she's here. She's waiting for us."

He shook his head. "She wasn't waiting for us. You saw her expression just like I did. She wasn't happy to see us, she—"

"She was surprised, that's all." My protest was just a tad too vehement because I was trying to convince him as well as myself. He was right. She hadn't exactly looked psyched to see us. If anything, she'd looked scared. That fear had been a punch in the gut coming from Ivy. She'd known us her whole life and knew we'd never, ever hurt her. The last time she'd seen us we'd made her come in the back of a truck, for Christ's sakes. Why would she be afraid of us?

Tonight, I aimed to find out. But first, I had to convince Cooper that we had a shot. "So maybe she wasn't as excited to see us as we'd hoped, but a lot of time has passed. Remember, she's not the same girl we knew either." No, she was so much more.

He was shaking his head before I finished. "It's not just that."

Ah hell. I recognized that intense look on his face. The nightmare must have messed with him because he'd gone someplace dark. Somewhere I wasn't going to be able to reach him, no matter how much I said.

"I've been thinking," he started.

Shit. I shifted in the booth, flagged down the waitress for more coffee. Whatever he'd been thinking, it couldn't have been good.

"I think we should let her go."

I stared at him in shocked silence. "Let her go?"

I shook my head and leaned forward again, far enough so he was forced to look at me. "She's the one. You know that as well as I do. We knew it the night in Baker's field. We wouldn't have touched her otherwise. We've been waiting *years* to have another shot with her and now...what? You want to quit before we've even begun?"

I saw a flash of guilt in his eyes and wanted to kick myself for giving him shit when he was already in a low place. "Where's this coming from?" I asked. "Why the change of heart?"

He scratched the back of his neck as he stared at the

eggs like they might leap off his plate. "I just...I don't know that I'm ready."

I was careful to school my features. If there was one thing I knew about my best friend, it was that he didn't want my pity. I knew exactly what he meant, of course, but I played dumb. "Not ready? I know for a fact you haven't been with a woman in ages." Since before the accident. Fuck, longer than that. There weren't women to fuck in the desert. I left that part unsaid as I gave him a teasing grin. "Are you telling me you didn't notice how hot she looked in that sundress?" I shifted in my seat, my cock at half-mast just thinking about the way the scooped neckline accentuated the soft curves of her breasts.

His grin was reluctant. "Of course, I noticed. Jesus, that woman is still as gorgeous as ever. More so." He fidgeted with his fork and I could see that he was switching tactics. The man was scared, and maybe rightfully so, but he had to get back to living his life. He had to move on and he had to do it with me and Ivy.

"Hard to believe she's not taken," he said.

No kidding. She was beautiful, smart, funny. Perfect. Why hadn't a man snatched her up by now?

Sure enough, Cooper was looking for an excuse to run away. Ivy was real. What we wanted with her was real. It wasn't a dream any longer. She wasn't a dream. A fantasy that I jerked off to in the shower. Not that I could blame him. Moving on was a lot harder for him than it was for me. The army had chewed us up and spit us out, but we had the rest of our lives ahead of us. No war. No bad guys. No IEDs or anti-aircraft fire.

I took a sip of my coffee. "I didn't see a wedding ring, did you?"

He shook his head. "That doesn't mean she's not dating someone."

"She said she wasn't," I countered.

"You saw the way she looked at us. Like we were ghosts or something. Clearly, she hasn't been pining over us these last seven years."

I shrugged, feigning a nonchalance I didn't feel. Too much was riding on this for me to take it lightly. "Seven years is a long time. Besides, so what if she hasn't pined for us, or whatever the fuck it's called? We never asked her to wait. We *wanted* her to go. We just didn't think it would be for this long. Besides, you know how it works as well as anyone. We know she's ours, now it's up to us to make her see that."

I'd spent half the night imagining just how we'd prove it to her. The last time we'd been with her, the sex had been great, but Lord knows we had no idea what we were doing. None of us had ever done it before. We'd been a bunch of fumbling virgins in the back of a pickup, but we'd made it good for her. Hell, it had been incredible to sink into her, to watch the arousal and need fill her eyes, to feel the way her body softened and took me in. The way she clenched and squeezed around my dick as she came. Again and again. The fact that she'd come for us, two fumbling teenagers, was a sign or something. It was *that good.*

Now, we were older, wiser, and well versed in the ways of pleasuring a woman. I knew where I wanted to start. That dress of hers had done little to conceal her tits, her nipples pressing against the thin material just begging to be sucked. I remembered their color, the way they'd tightened in my mouth. The whole time we'd been talking to her, a little part of my brain couldn't stop obsessing over what she wore underneath the sundress. Clearly there was no bra. But had she been wearing panties? If so, were they lacy? Pink? A fucking thong so her perfect ass was bare?

"Earth to Rory." Cooper was watching me and I forced my brain to come back from its dirty wandering and focus on my best friend, who still looked like he had the weight of the world on his shoulders. "Look, if she's happy with her life, I don't know that we should be coming in and—"

"Fuck that." I tempered my voice so the other tables didn't hear my swearing. "I refuse to listen to any more of your stupid excuses." I set my mug of coffee down on the table. "She's ours, we're not just going to let her walk away from us again. Not now when we have something to offer her."

"What do I have to offer?" His voice was hoarse and filled with unspoken emotions that made my chest ache on his behalf. "Seriously, Rory, I'd like to know...what the hell do you think I can give Ivy?"

I opened my mouth to answer, but he wasn't done.

"She hasn't been waiting all these years so she can settle down with a broken man who can't even sleep through the night like a normal person. She can't be interested in a man that killed more than a handful of men."

"Fuck that shit." I tried to meet his gaze but he was looking everywhere but at me, like he was too ashamed to face me. I leaned forward and dropped my voice so the rest of the restaurant didn't hear. "The chopper crash wasn't your fault." They were words I said often enough, but until he believed them, it wouldn't make a bit of fucking difference. "I know you're going through hell, man. But you're getting better every day, physically and in every other way. Ivy liked you just fine before. She's not a bitch. She's not looking for perfect. She never was. She's looking for us, the guys who claimed her that night."

"We're not the same."

"No, we're not. We're better. Smarter. Wiser. Know the shit that's out there and will keep her safe."

He gave a small nod but I knew he wasn't hearing me.

I fell back in my seat with a sigh. "I know it's not easy. Shit, maybe it never will be. What happened to you won't go away and it will never be right, but it will get a little easier with time. Isn't that what the doctors are always telling you?"

The corner of his mouth turned up in a minor semblance of a smile, but he didn't respond.

"I know for a fact that it was thoughts of Ivy that pulled you through in the hospital. I fucking heard you call out her name." I watched his reaction and he gave me a grudging nod of agreement. He'd made me talk about her and relive that night with him countless times after the accident. When he got tired of reminiscing about her smile, her hair, her scent, the feel of her pussy...that's when we'd switch to talking about how it could be. How it *would* be once we got her back. And we were getting her back. He just needed to get his head out of his ass long enough to do so.

Cooper's smile grew and I knew he was remembering the plans we'd made for our future home with our gorgeous wife. "That was a good dream."

"It was more than a dream, Cooper. It's our fucking destiny, and you know it. We've found her. Seen her. Even made a damn date with her. Don't you dare give up on that now when we're so close."

For the first time in a long time, he gave me a real smile. Not rueful or self-deprecating, but an honest-to-God genuine grin. "Yeah, all right. Let's go get our girl."

Damn straight.

4

*I*VY

My aunt stared at me like I was a crazy person and I couldn't blame her. I was standing by the front door, shifting from one foot to the other as I called upstairs to Lily for the third time. "Come on, hon, you're going to be late."

Aunt Sarah tipped her head to the side as she peered at me through her bifocals. In her late seventies, she was my second mother. Since my real one didn't count, Grandma was first. Then, when she passed, Aunt Sarah had definitely filled that role. And boy, had I needed someone. Eighteen and pregnant? I couldn't have done it without her. While her hair was still long—she refused to cut it and have helmet-head like an old lady—she'd decided to let the gray show. Even though she'd grown up in Bridgewater, she didn't dress like a cowgirl. In fact, I'd never seen her in jeans. Her style was simple, with bright colors and bold jewelry.

She looked at the watch on her slim wrist. "The movie doesn't start for an hour, Ivy. We've got plenty of time."

I tried to force a smile but I was pretty sure it came off as a grimace. I needed them gone. Out. Far, far away. And I needed it now. I'd been on a few dates, but this wasn't a *real* date. This was Cooper and Rory. There was no comparison. Dates were namby-pamby men who brought flowers and took me to a restaurant with an all-you-can-eat salad bar and kissed my cheek at the end of the night. Cooper and Rory? They were...indescribable.

Aunt Sarah still watched me, sizing me up from my peep-toe heels to my sexy dress. The dress was little and black, and I referred to it as my "sexy dress" on the few occasions that I'd worn it. It was the only one in my closet that didn't look like it was meant for parent/teacher night at school and that in and of itself made it sexy.

"Do you have a date tonight?" Aunt Sarah asked.

Date! No, I was having dinner with the two men who'd claimed me, body and soul, seven years ago and left me to live my dream. And gave me Lily.

I wasn't entirely sure how to respond to that while being truthful. This morning, when I'd asked her to watch Lily for me, I'd told her I had plans tonight. I'd specifically said *plans* and not *date* for this very reason. The butterflies in my stomach went wild at the word "date." That one-syllable made my knees weak and my breathing uneven. Holy cow, it had been way too long since I'd been out with a man. And tonight I was going out with two men. Two insanely hot, ridiculously sexy men. Two men who'd fucked me senseless and looked at me like they'd like to do it again.

But this was *not* a date, I reminded myself. Again. This was a catch up with old friends. It was a way for me to make it clear that I'd moved on. I would be firm, but polite. They meant nothing to me. Yeah, right.

Aunt Sarah waited for a response.

"Not exactly a date," I mumbled before turning back to holler for Lily once more.

When I turned around, she was eyeing my outfit that screamed *date,* but fortunately she remained quiet.

Ten minutes later they were finally out the door, Lily tucked happily in her booster to see the movie she'd been talking about all week. Thank the Lord. This night would be nerve wracking enough without Cooper and Rory running into Lily when they picked me up in...oh holy crap. Five minutes. I scanned the hallway and the kitchen. Toys were strewn as far as the eye could see. Pink girlie stuff everywhere. There was no way I'd scour this place of all signs of a child before they arrived. I grabbed my wrap and purse from the hallway table and went out to the porch. I just wouldn't invite them in, that was all.

I'd been on a few dates over the years and one thing I could say about Bridgewater men...they knew how to do it right. Cooper and Rory arrived right on time. And with flowers.

Even though I was prepared to see them this time, my heart still went into overdrive when they came up the walk. They both wore button-down shirts and fitted pants. Their hair was neat, their faces clean-shaven. They still had that rugged, almost dangerous look about them. "You boys, um... look nice." Crap, was that my voice? It sounded breathy, like I was a phone sex worker or something.

"You look amazing." Cooper handed me the flowers and gave me a kiss on the cheek that made my lungs stop working. Never one to be outdone, Rory came to my side and placed a hand on my waist before giving me a chaste kiss as well. My skin tingled where their lips had touched. God, what would it be like if they got me naked and not standing outside on my front porch in broad daylight?

They were both in my personal space, their heat sheltering me from the soft breeze and their scent...oh Lord, that scent. The air was filled with that earthy, manly smell that made my lower belly feel heavy and my skin tingle. It was just as I remembered it from all those years ago.

That was when I knew—there was no way I could survive an entire night with these two. Not without either losing my mind or dropping my panties. For years, I'd been telling myself that their effect on me back in high school could be chalked up to teenage hormones. I hadn't felt anything else like it ever since.

But now...it was back. The feel of Rory's hand on my waist was enough to make my pussy throb. And if Cooper didn't stop looking at me like that—like he was going to throw me down and fuck me on the front porch—I might lose all control and start begging for it.

I'd made a mistake. A monumental mistake. I should never have said yes to this date...or non-date...or whatever this was. I wasn't strong enough. My resistance was weak. My heart, it was too damn fragile.

"Let me...um, let me put these flowers in water. I'll be right back."

I dashed into the kitchen, filled a pitcher I used for lemonade from under the sink and put the flowers in. I'd tend to them later. Taking a deep breath, I returned to the men on the porch, locked the door behind me.

"Shall we?" Rory took a step back and offered me his arm. I looked at the bent elbow, the muscles that played beneath the fabric of his shirt. My mouth went dry and that was just his *arm*.

There was no turning back now. They were waiting patiently. I owed it to myself, to women everywhere, to take this one night with them. I'd thought about this for years. I'd kick myself. No, I'd probably kill myself if I walked inside and shut the door on them. One night. Just *one*. How hard could it be?

I placed my hand in the crook of his elbow and discovered Rory was *hard*. Very hard and I had to wonder if that was all over. God, I had the mind of a slut.

Even the car ride was difficult for me, being in the closed space with them, breathing them in, listening to the rough timbre of their voices. Luckily, they kept a steady stream of conversation going because my brain had officially turned to mush in the presence of so much testosterone.

I hadn't remembered Rory as the chatty one, but he talked most of the way to the restaurant, filling me in on the goings-on in Bridgewater and asking questions about my home, my job. I found myself giving him one-word answers because I was so nervous about revealing too much. Lily was my whole world. It was nearly impossible to talk about my life without mentioning her, so my only option was not to talk.

Things got a little easier once we sat down to dinner. They'd chosen a lovely restaurant. Not too fancy, but it had an outdoor patio that overlooked the water. I'd never been before, but had heard it was good. Eating out with a six-year-old took me to different places, mostly ones that served food quickly and had macaroni and cheese on the menu. This place? They wanted their guests to linger. The wine helped me calm down, as well as the people around us. It was easier to ignore the men's' heated looks and their heady scent when a waiter was standing next to me refilling my water glass or an elderly couple beside us started talking a little too loudly.

By the time the main course arrived, I was almost feeling like myself again. The butterflies had calmed down some and I stopped freezing up every time they asked me a question about my life. I also felt more comfortable asking them about their lives over the past seven years and listened in awe as they told me about their experiences in the military. Rory did most of the talking about that and he quickly glossed over their last tour and discharge from the army.

I noticed Cooper's jaw clench and his body tense, but he took a deep breath, finally spoke. "We're here because we've missed you, Ivy," Cooper said, lifting his arm to indicate the restaurant, perhaps even Seattle. The topic change was surprising. I wasn't sure if it was because he no longer wanted to talk about their time in the service—it seemed it set him on edge—or if he *really* wanted to talk about us. Or lack of us. Or...crap, a *possibility* of an us.

He leaned forward slightly and reached for my hand, took it. I could have pulled away, but I didn't. It was large and warm as it enveloped mine. I felt the callouses, the roughness of the life he'd led in just his palm.

The simple words should have scared me. *We've missed you.*

They not only didn't scare me, they made my chest expand like my heart was about to take flight. I longed to hear them, to know that they'd been longing for me as much as I had for them. Maybe that was why I didn't respond right away. I had a whole speech prepared, but it went unspoken as I met Cooper's gaze. I couldn't look away from the intensity, the longing.

After too much time passed, Rory reached for my other

hand so I was trapped between the two of them. He gave me a smoldering look that had me squirming in my seat to relieve the ache. Yes, these two made me ache. Just hearing them admit they'd missed me made me ache.

"Say something, sweets."

Sweets. The term of endearment sounded so natural coming out of his mouth and brought back so many memories.

I said the first coherent thought that passed through my mind. "I've missed you, too."

Cooper's smile of relief brought with it a stab of guilt that nearly made me panic. Shit, that wasn't what I was supposed to say. It was the truth, but it wasn't right. But the way he looked after I said it? It was as if he took in the sun.

"I missed you, but..." I struggled to remember what I'd planned to say. "But this can't happen."

Cooper's face fell, but Rory looked unfazed. "And why's that?"

"Do you have a boyfriend?" Cooper asked when I didn't immediately answer.

I should have said yes. That would have been the easy way out. But I'd never been much of a liar and I missed the opportunity. I'd waited too long and they could see the truth of it in my expression. They'd always been able to read me and now that was dangerous.

"There's no one else, is there?" Rory confirmed. They'd asked this the day before, but obviously they thought it was worth repeating. I respected them more for it; they would have backed off if my heart was given to someone else.

I shook my head because my heart had always belonged to them. Not that I was going to tell them *that*.

He raised my hand to his lips as if rewarding me for my

honesty and I felt that simple gentle kiss all the way to my toes. My skin tingled and my nipples instantly hardened.

Cooper's brow furrowed as he studied me. "Then what's the problem?"

I licked my lips, a move that had both their gazes fixed on my mouth. Inhaling deeply, I said a quick prayer for strength. "My life is...it's complicated."

Rory nodded like that made perfect sense. "We've all grown up, sweets. We all have issues and problems, but that's no reason not to give us a shot, is it?"

Cooper hurried to talk before I could come up with another protest. "Trust me, your issues are nothing like mine and I'm here, right? We're not asking you to commit to us right now. We know you have a life here in Seattle and we respect that."

I frowned. "Then what are you asking?" I couldn't help myself. I had to know. The temptation was too great.

"Give us tonight," Rory said quietly. His eyes were dark and his intent clear. "All night."

I met his gaze and oh, holy shit. That was the sexiest look I'd ever seen. He made no attempt to hide his desire or the meaning behind those two words.

"All night?" I had no idea why I repeated it, perhaps just wanting to hear it again. It made my mind go to some deliciously dirty places. Oh, the things I could do with those hard, muscular bodies...all night long.

Cooper must have seen what the thought of it was doing to me, because he took it one step further. Placing a hand on my knee under the table he stroked the sensitive skin there, just below the hem of my dress. I startled, but relaxed into the warmth of his palm. I hadn't been touched by a man intimately in a long, long time and it just felt good. My body seemed to recognize them, their touch. "Just one night, sweets, so we can remind you of how good it is between the three of us. And we're not eighteen anymore, nor virgins."

I bit my lip to hold back a laugh. Did they really think I'd forgotten how good it had been? That even though it had been the first time for all of us, it had been really, really good. Hell, I remembered how amazing it had been when I spent some quality time with my vibrator. I'd relived that night every day for the past seven years.

And now...well, now I was being offered the chance to truly relive that night. For real, not just in my imagination. I had no doubt it would be even better than I remembered because Cooper was right. They weren't eighteen anymore and I itched—no, ached—to get my hands on those hard muscles.

I might have tossed myself into their arms right then and there if I hadn't caught a flicker of hope along with the heat in Cooper's eyes. If I said yes, they'd take it to mean more. They'd been clear with me from the start that they thought I was the one, and I knew that I wasn't. That I couldn't be, not anymore.

I'd given up any dreams of a happily ever after with these guys the day I decided to keep our baby and raise her on my own. Her. *Lily.* "One night wouldn't change anything." Even I could hear the regret in my voice. The wistfulness. The need.

Rory leaned forward, his gaze intent. "Let us worry about that." Before I could argue, he hurried on. "We're not asking you to make any kind of commitment. This one night would be just that—one night. No strings attached."

I studied his earnest expression. "But you want more. You've made that clear."

"We do want more," Cooper answered, his low voice filled with honesty. He squeezed his fingers on my leg. "But we'll take what we can get. And right now, all we're asking for is tonight."

I tried to come up with more arguments, but my mind was having a hard time functioning under their heated stares. Cooper's hand moved a touch higher up my thigh and all of my attention was focused on the feel of his rough, calloused fingers against the soft skin. I wondered how it would feel if he touched my inner thigh, and then up further...

I reached for my glass of wine and drained it in one gulp. But the tart liquid did nothing to stop the aching in my core. My pussy was wet and throbbing, and for one desperate moment I thought about catching his hand, placing it over my needy pussy right then and there. *Easy, girl.*

I didn't know if Rory could read my mind or if he just saw the telltale flush in my cheeks, but he reached a hand out and placed it on my other leg, firmly gripping my upper thigh. A little squeaking noise escaped from my throat.

Oh God, my level of horniness was almost embarrassing. I hadn't gone out much since Lily was born, but I hadn't become a nun. Still, none of those encounters had left me this hot and ready, and Rory and Cooper were just touching my legs. And in public, although beneath the long hem of the tablecloth. I could only imagine what would happen if I went back to bed with them. I'd probably come before they got my dress off.

With his free hand, Rory lifted mine and brought it to his lips. "What do you have to lose, sweets?" His lips brushed against the underside of my wrist, making me shiver.

What did I have to lose? *Everything.* A panicky voice in the back of my mind told me I'd be playing with fire, letting these guys back into my life. *But it was just one night,* another voice argued. Those words weren't so much coming from my brain as was my pussy. If it was just one night, maybe I didn't have anything to lose. They said themselves that this was all they would take. After tonight, if I told them to leave, they'd have to go. If there was one thing I'd never doubted, it was that these men had integrity. They wouldn't lie about that. If I told them to hit the road tomorrow morning, I'd never see them again. The thought was bittersweet and made me swallow. Hard.

One night didn't seem like nearly enough with these two —it hadn't been seven years ago—but it was the best I could ever hope for. I could never have more than that—not without risking Lily's stability and everything we'd built. But I could have tonight. A taste of the kind of passion my life was currently missing. The man-induced orgasms. Being with Rory and Cooper again and giving me enough fantasy fodder to last me another seven years.

Cooper's hand slid up beneath my dress so both men had a proprietary grip on my inner thighs, forcing me to part my legs slightly to accommodate. I glanced about to see if anyone took notice of what was happening beneath our table, but no one was paying us any attention.

Rory moved first, his fingers inching up until they brushed against my panties, making me gasp. Then Cooper followed his lead until they were both stroking me through the soaking wet material.

I took a quick glance around the restaurant but no one was looking our way and the tablecloth obscured what was going on underneath.

Cooper and Rory shared a quick grin as Rory said, "Now there's no way you can deny that you're tempted by the offer." He leaned in, whispered, "You're dripping wet and now we both know it."

Cooper made a little growl and I flicked my gaze to his. Yes, that was the look I remembered. Intense, but the slight turn of his lips promised fun, too.

I bit my lip to hold back a moan as one of his fingers slipped beneath the silky material of my panties and between the folds of my pussy. It was almost impossible to keep from moaning and calling attention to our table. When his fingers slipped inside of me, my hips bucked involuntarily trying to get closer. Heat flared through me. Cooper made a soothing sound like he was dealing with a startled colt as his fingers found my clit and stroked it mercilessly.

I didn't remember it feeling like this in the back of the pick-up. *Oh God. Oh holy shit.* My guys were going to make me come in the middle of a freaking restaurant.

I jerked my chair back so quickly the tables next to us finally took notice. My breath came in gasps and I was fairly certain my face was so flushed it must have looked like I'd just run a marathon.

Rory and Cooper were smirking but the look in their eyes was heated. They weren't unaffected.

Cooper lifted his fingers to his mouth, licked them, one by one.

They knew how quickly I'd responded, how needy I was, how badly I wanted this.

How wet I was.

I was practically shaking with pent up desire and it was messing with my mind. For the life of me, I couldn't remember why I was fighting them on this. Why didn't I want them to make me come? I obviously didn't want to do so in the middle of the restaurant, but in a bed, with one of them on either side of me. My pussy was more than eager. It ached to be filled by their thick cocks. I ached to be touched. Why didn't I want to spend a hot night with them?

It was just *one night*. My ovaries were jumping for joy at the idea, my nipples hard points, my panties ruined. What could it hurt? Well, it could hurt my heart, but I wanted a night. I wanted them again. I wanted to relive what we'd had, what we'd shared, even if it was going to be over in the morning.

I wanted Cooper's fingers again. Their cocks. Their mouths. Everything.

"Okay," I said, licking my lips as nerves made my mouth go dry.

5

*I*VY

Oh God, I was doing this. I was really going to do this. My pussy clenched at what was going to happen, what they were going to do. I remembered that one night, but we'd only been eighteen then. Now? Now, I had to make sure I didn't black out when they made me come, because what they'd done with their fingers beneath the table? That was just the beginning.

I moved my chair back some more so I could stand. Ever the gentlemen, they made a move to stand as well but I stopped them with the palm of my hand. I saw a mix of frustration and understanding in their gazes. They were just as eager as I was but I doubted they had butterflies in their stomachs like me. No, they had hard dicks in their pants. "Just...just give me a minute."

When I reached the waiting area I stopped to catch my

breath before calling Aunt Sarah, fumbling with the phone to do so. I was all wound up, nervous, flustered. A hot, horny mess. I told her I was having fun and might be home late. Much to my chagrin, she sounded way too excited about that, even happily offering to put Lily to bed and read her the nightly story. She must have insisted ten times that I shouldn't feel the need to rush home tonight, or even tomorrow morning.

She knew what I was going to do and giving me the go-ahead. She wanted me to get it on with a date, or two. That was pretty embarrassing—my life was clearly dull to observers if Aunt Sarah was all but pushing me into sleeping around. She was actively encouraging me to have sex!

No, I wasn't sleeping around. I was sleeping with Rory and Cooper. These weren't strangers I picked up in a bar. They were the two I'd wanted my whole life. I was doing this. I was going to take those two hot cowboys for a ride.

I hurried back to the table, eagerness and excitement making me tremble in a whole new way. Rory was signing the check when I reached them. They stood and Rory came to my side, put his hand at the small of my back and led me toward the door.

"What about dessert?" I teased.

"You're our dessert." Rory's low voice right next to my ear gave me goosebumps and had my thoughts switching to them licking me. Everywhere.

I glanced at Cooper in confusion when they were steering me away from the exit that led to the parking lot. "Where are you taking me?"

Cooper grinned, the corner of his mouth tipped up. I had to wonder why he had interest in *me* when he turned women's heads everywhere he went with that smile. It was like a woman-magnet and no woman in a thirty-foot radius was immune, me included. "This restaurant adjoins our hotel. We're going up to Rory's room."

My mouth fell open for a second before I burst out with a laugh. There was no way this was coincidence. "Wow, you brought me back to your hotel for dinner? Someone was feeling awfully sure of himself tonight."

"We both were," Cooper said, his hand gripping my elbow and steering me toward an elevator bank.

"Do you guys really think I'm that easy?" I was teasing but they must have caught the underlying insecurity in my tone because they both came to a stop and turned to me. Rory cupped my face in the palm of his hand, his eyes darkening with intensity.

"Easy? Hell, no. Seven years of wondering where you were is pretty hard-to-get. We have the highest respect for you, sweets. Don't ever forget that." He dropped a light kiss on my lips and a ridiculous wave of emotions had tears stinging the back of my eyes.

"There's no denying the chemistry between the three of us," he continued. "We all feel the connection. You aren't a quick fuck. You're it for us."

I longed to hear those words, but they scared the crap out of me. I nodded though, because I had to admit they were right. We did have chemistry, although it was more like TNT. I wasn't so sure I was it for them, though. I didn't want to give them false hope. They watched me now with such sweet concern, clearly still worried I felt disrespected. But I didn't. No, I felt wanted and when Rory stepped close, pressed the hard length of his cock against my side, I felt *very* wanted. My pussy clenched again in anticipation.

I was doing this. I'd live the rest of my life with regret if I didn't.

Now that I'd made my decision, I was all in. This was what I wanted. *They* were what I wanted. I'd have my one night of bliss and then I'd send them on their way. That same bittersweet pang made my heart ache, but I ignored it as I smiled up at them. "If this connection is so strong, what the hell are we waiting for?"

Cooper let out a short laugh and linked my arm through his once more so he could lead me toward the elevator, Rory following close behind. Rory hit the number for his floor and both men turned to face me.

Oh holy hell. I'd forgotten how intense they could be, how overwhelming it was when they both looked at me like that. Like I was the sun and the moon and an all-you-could-eat buffet all in one. The adoration in their eyes was humbling. And that ravenous hunger...well, I was certain they saw the same in my gaze.

"I don't think I can wait till we get to the room to get my hands on this sweet body," Cooper said, his voice a rough growl. "How about you, Rory?"

Rory shook his head slowly, his eyes fastened on me. Reaching up, he brushed my hair back, tucked it behind my ear. That, followed by a gentle caress of his knuckles down my exposed cheek made my eyes fall closed. "Nope. We've been waiting too long. I definitely can't wait any longer. And you got a taste of that pussy," he grumbled, clearly mad that Cooper had licked my arousal from his fingers and Rory hadn't.

Cavemen.

They moved in closer—I felt their body heat radiating off them—and I fought for air as their meaning struck. My eyes flew up and I was in a mild panic. "Here? You guys, we're in an elevator. You can't go down on me here." I glanced at the brushed nickel walls. "We could be caught."

"Just another taste," Cooper murmured.

The rest of my protests flew out of my mind as his lips found the sensitive skin behind my ear. My head fell back against the elevator wall and my lips parted. Rory took advantage, licking at my lower lip before thrusting his tongue into my mouth, making me moan. This was what I remembered, the feel of them surrounding me, possessing me. And we were fully clothed in an elevator. What was it going to feel like once we were in bed and naked?

Their hands were everywhere, skimming over my legs and hips, cupping my ass, and massaging my breasts. I was whimpering by the time the elevator came to a stop with a ding. I straightened quickly, terrified that other passengers were about to get on, but when the doors slid open, Rory stepped back and gestured for me to step off first. I was impressed at how civilized he became from one second to the next. "This is my floor."

The moment his hotel room door closed behind us though, we were at it again, this time with a desperation that was heady and overwhelming. I fumbled with their clothes as they continued their kissing and nibbling. I only had two hands to strip two hard bodies and made a sound of frustration against Rory's lips. He pulled back and I managed to say, "I need to see you."

"Yes, ma'am," Cooper said with a sly grin.

They made quick work of shedding their clothes. Rory pulled a condom from the pocket of his pants and tossed it on the bed. Good, while I had an IUD, I remembered last time and knew exactly how virile they were. I took a step away from them so I could take it in, this mouthwatering array of brawn and muscle. Rory stood before me in nothing, his cock long and thick and pointing straight at me. A dark and dangerous gleam shone in his eyes as he waited for me to look my fill. There was no embarrassment—he had zero modesty it seemed, but it was no wonder with his military-honed physique. He looked like he was tensed, ready to pounce. I just had to curl my finger.

But I wanted to see Cooper, too. To take in the men they'd become, every bare, hard inch. He'd shed his pants, but was lingering over his button-down shirt. His earlier bravado seemed to have faded. I went over to help him and for a second he froze when my hands went to push the shirt over his broad shoulders. I saw something I hadn't expected. Worry. Apprehension. "Fair warning, sweets. I'm not the man I was."

I frowned, expecting him to say more, but he didn't. Because of this, I waited, my hands poised in the air until he nodded, to give me consent to see something he wanted hidden. Letting out a long sigh as the shirt dropped, I quickly saw why he'd hesitated. Scars covered his left arm and upper chest. These weren't marks of a small wound or childhood injury. No, this was a remnant of war. Battle. Evil. By the size and number of scars, he was lucky to be alive.

My chest squeezed painfully at the visible sign of all the pain he'd suffered. He hadn't told me much, just skimmed over what had happened to him at dinner. Said he'd been in an accident which was why he was discharged from the military, but he didn't tell me the extent. I just assumed the information was classified or something. Not this. He didn't want to tell me he'd almost given his life for his country.

I wasn't letting this get between us, to affect what we had. To me, he was perfect. I was attracted to him, scars and all.

I touched him gently, tentatively, felt the thick edges of

the scarring, the way it was pink and tender looking beside his unmarred tan skin. But then he grabbed my hand and pressed it to his chest, telling me without words that my touch didn't hurt him. They might not give him physical pain, but it was obvious he hadn't recovered from the emotional pain of his accident. I leaned in and kissed one of the scars and heard his quick intake of air before his hands tangled in my hair and held me close, his lips pressing against the side of my head.

I didn't care about the scars, only that he'd endured so much pain from them. I saw *him,* not the healed wounds. They only showed that he'd survived, that he'd been brave and strong. They were badges of honor and I kissed each one.

"I'm wet for you," I admitted. He sucked in a breath at my bold words. "You felt it. If you don't believe my words, believe my body, my desire."

He groaned then, pulling me in to him, all the tension seeping out of him. Rory came up behind me and Cooper eased his grip, but tilted my head up so he could claim my mouth.

I felt the emotion, the need in that kiss. He'd been worried I'd think less of him and I felt all of his concerns melt away as his mouth moved over mine, as his tongue plunged deep, just as I hoped his cock would soon enough. But they seemed to have no interest to take me fast. Dammit. I wiggled, rubbing back and forth against both of them. I heard a growl from Rory, but they didn't take the hint and toss me on the bed and fuck me senseless.

No, these men wanted foreplay.

Rory wrapped his arms around me from behind, his muscles pressing against my back and his hard cock nestled against my ass. Cooper pulled me closer so my breasts molded to his chest, his cock jutting against my lower belly. I didn't have to doubt their eagerness and when they got me naked, they'd find I was more eager than ever. My panties were ruined.

My little black dress was all that separated me from these men. *My men.* Their hard bodies had me trapped between them and I'd never in my life had felt so safe. So treasured. Not even that one night we'd shared so long ago. I let myself revel in the sensation as they kissed my lips and neck.

But then the frustration grew to be too much. In a matter of seconds, they had me back to the painfully turned on state I'd been in when we were in the restaurant. My dress was in the way, keeping me from what I wanted. It wasn't enough. I needed *more.*

"Cooper," I breathed against his lips. Begged.

"What do you need?" he murmured. I felt his warm breath fan my heated skin.

"You." I looked over my shoulder at Rory. "Both of you."

"It's our turn to see you," he said, stepping back. With deft fingers, Cooper pulled my dress over my head and Rory unfastened my bra. When my breasts fell free, they both groaned. Rory turned me so I stood between them, so they could both get their first bare glimpse of me since I was eighteen and in the back of Cooper's truck.

For the first time since they'd started kissing me, a new sort of fear took hold and held me in its grip. I bit my lip and held my breath. Could they see a difference? My breasts definitely weren't as perky as they once were. Gravity and breastfeeding had taken their toll. What if I didn't live up to their expectations? I was in fairly good shape, but I'd had a baby—my body was different, definitely not the tight, hot body of a high school senior. And not the tight, hot pussy of an inexperienced teen, either. If they looked close enough, they'd see the faded, silver lines of my stretch marks.

I moved a hand to cover my belly, but Rory brushed it gently aside with impatience. "Don't hide from us, sweets. We've been dreaming about this moment for far too long. To see you bare before us again. Between us. To know you want us just as much as we do you. Your panties are soaked."

I blushed at his carnal words. "You knew that already," I countered, then swallowed down the nerves that made me want to tell them everything. To bare more than my body.

"You are so fucking gorgeous," Cooper muttered as he lowered his head to suck on one hard nipple. I gave a small cry as his lips firmed and I felt the gentle pull. I grabbed the back of his head and held him to me as he moved between my breasts, covering them in kisses and teasing my nipples until I was panting for air. They were more sensitive than I ever imagined.

"You look even better than I remembered," Rory said as he came back behind me and wrapped me in his arms, his hands sliding up and down my sides. "How is that possible?"

I shook my head, but didn't say a word. I couldn't. All I could do was moan when Cooper cupped my breasts with his palms, licking and nibbling with his mouth, teasing with his fingers. My anxiety faded with each pull of his mouth, with every whispered word from Rory's lips.

My head fell back against Rory's shoulder as he lowered his hand to cup my pussy through my panties. When I moaned, he bent his knees slightly and nudged my legs apart so he could nestle his cock between my thighs.

This time, we both moaned. It was so intimate, yet such a tease since I still wore my silk panties. "I need it. I need your cock in me," I said, not caring I was so bold with my words. "I can't wait any longer."

That was the truth. My pussy was aching for it. I needed to feel them inside of me.

Rory gave my shoulder a little love bite before taking a step back, grabbing the condom, ripping it open and rolling it on before coming back. Sheathed and ready, he tugged my panties down to my ankles. I stepped out of them and he nudged my legs apart once more to position himself right at my entrance. His cock slid inside of me in one hard, slow thrust. My eyes widened and I met Cooper's heated gaze as Rory stretched me open, filled me deep. Took me slow. I cried out at the delicious feel of being claimed by Rory as Cooper held me upright, continuing to play with my breasts as Rory fucked me from behind. I gripped Cooper's forearms, thankful he was there to keep me upright.

Foreplay was over. They hadn't even taken me to bed, just fucked me right inside the doorway.

I was so ready, so primed by them, it only took three thrusts of Rory's thick cock before I came in their arms, my cries of pleasure cutting through the silence of the hotel room. I had no idea it could be like this, so desperate, sweaty, wild. I'd never fucked standing up before, never like this.

They covered me with kisses as I came back to earth. Murmured words of praise, affection. I might have come once, but this night was far from over. Rory was still deep inside me. He hadn't come and I felt him thick and hard, so deep his hips pressed against my ass. His voice was a growl in my ear as he pulled out. He groaned and I whimpered. "No," I whispered, not wanting him to leave me. I felt empty without him.

Cooper spun me about, my breasts swaying with the motion. Rory nodded toward the bed. "On your hands and knees."

The curt command made me hot all over again. I liked this bossy side of him, that he was taking from me what he wanted. I could say no and he'd stop. They both would. But why? I knew however they took me, fast or slow, wild or passionate, they'd make me come. Again and again. My pussy clenched with sweet anticipation.

I hurried over to the bed and positioned myself how he'd demanded. Rory came to the edge of the bed, his cock at my eye level. He'd stripped off the condom as I'd moved. Jesus, he was hung. Thick, gorgeous.

Cooper got onto the bed behind me and I heard him open a condom. I had no idea where it came from, but I didn't care. The men were prepared and were taking care of me, in more ways than one. Before I could think anything more of it, he gripped my hip, slid a hand soothingly down my spine.

"Ready for both of us, sweets?"

I looked back at Cooper, saw his cock primed and ready for his turn, then looked up at Rory. His hand gripped the base of his cock and he leaned toward me. I licked my lips, then opened wide, ready for both my men.

Some would say it was crazy having a threesome, that there was something wrong with it. But I was raised in Bridgewater, knew where I stood with these two—even if I fought it tooth and nail—and wanted them both. What we did was hot. Steamy. Wild. But it was...special. They weren't just fucking me, they were claiming me all over again.

They entered me at the same time. Rory slipped his cock into my open mouth and Cooper worked his cock into my pussy with hard, deliberate strokes.

That one night I hadn't sucked either of them off, all of us too busy fucking for the first time to do it. But Rory's taste

VANESSA VALE

had my mouth watering. He was careful with how much he fed me, pulling back and rocking into me with easy strokes.

Cooper fucked with a deliberation and intensity not shared by Rory. He held me right where he wanted me, the broad head hitting every sweet spot deep inside me. He knew just how to move, to take me to make me come again.

It was an urgent and mind-blowing give and take. Each of us focused on pleasuring the other. Sucking and licking and fucking and touching until all three of us came apart. Rory's seed spilled down my throat and Cooper deep in my pussy, filling the condom. No baby this time. Lily wasn't a mistake. She was the light of my life, but I wasn't ready for another. I was only ready for another round with my two hot cowboys. Round two was enough for now.

They took me three more times throughout the night, in between some much-needed bouts of rest. The last time I woke, the sun was starting to come in through the slit in the closed drapes and my heart sank at the sight. I felt both men on either side of me, Rory's arm slung over my waist, his palm cupping my breast. Cooper was asleep in front of me, his thigh brushing mine. They seemed to want constant contact as much as me.

This was it. My one night in heaven was over. This dirty Cinderella's coach was about to turn into a pumpkin. I ached to remain between them, to feel safe and protected, cherished and... theirs.

But no. It wasn't just me anymore. I couldn't be selfish or greedy. Moms couldn't do that.

I tried to be quiet as I got out of bed, and slipped into my bra and little black dress from the night before. My panties were on the floor, ruined. Rory and Cooper were better than I remembered. Smart, kind. Funny. Generous and brave. Hot as could be and very skilled at pleasuring me. All different kinds of ways. But that wasn't enough. I glanced back at them in bed, the space between them obvious. Tears stung the back of my eyes at the thought of having to say goodbye. Again.

For good this time.

6

OOPER

I shook Rory awake as I watched our girl get ready to flee. Yeah, fucking flee. She was going to leave without waking us as if what we'd done was shameful.

I had to admit I was surprised. Hurt, even. We'd had an amazing night and I knew she'd felt it, too. She hadn't been faking, not when her pussy walls had rippled as she came, her nipples hardened against my tongue. I hadn't missed the way she'd clawed at Rory's shoulders as he ate her out.

That old connection, the sizzling heat, was still there. It was better than ever, this thing between us. We might have been teenagers before, but we'd known Ivy was the one. That hadn't changed and last night proved it. Even to me, who'd been so fucking doubtful. Scared of what she'd say about my scars. I'd been wrong. So damn wrong. We had a chance to be with her, a really good chance. No military, no college between us and Rory and I were going to do everything we could to keep her.

When we'd finally fallen asleep, I hadn't dreamed, I hadn't woken in a cold sweat, the chopper falling out of the sky again. No, I'd slept the best I had in a long time with Ivy in my arms.

While I'd known it would be amazing, having her beneath us again, we'd needed her to see it. And she had, I was sure of it. But obviously only in the short term. We'd said one night and she'd taken it to heart. Not one night to show her what it could be like, what it *would* be like if she let us. No, she was one and done. But why? Why walk away from something so good?

Why the hell was she running out of here like the devil was on her tail?

I heard Rory roll over, the empty expanse of bed wide between us where Ivy should have been. "What's going on?" he murmured as he blinked sleep from his eyes. I knew the moment he caught sight of a guilty looking Ivy slipping on her heels because he sat upright beside me. "Where are you going?"

She glanced at us and her face was pale, stricken. Her eyes looked sad, haunted.

I sat up too, leaned against the headboard, my eyes focused on the details—the way her hands shook slightly as she fumbled with her earrings. The way she bit her lip and refused to make eye contact.

She didn't want to leave. She'd been just as affected. The realization struck me with force and gave me hope, which was a rare feeling for me these days. I hadn't fucking felt it in a long, long time. I'd stopped being hopeful nearly a year ago when I'd survived the accident of my making when so many others hadn't. Optimism wasn't something I believed in anymore...not until now. Not until Ivy.

The way I was raised was too ingrained in me. We might not be in Bridgewater, but the customs deeply rooted there remained with me. With Rory. She was the one. She was ours. I knew it to be true, just like I knew that it was meant to be. It took seeing her again, being with her, *in her,* for me to remember the beliefs I'd been raised with. That I wanted to share for the rest of my life.

"You don't have to go," I said quietly, trying not to spook her any more than she already was. That's the way it seemed, at least. I recognized that look in her eyes. It was fear and regret. She wanted to stay, so what the hell was keeping her from us?

She might have looked rattled, but she also had an air of determination about her. Her jaw was set and her lips pressed together like she was ready for battle. There was no way we were getting her to talk, not that her efforts to get dressed and out the door were deterring Rory from asking a million questions.

"Do you need a ride home? When can we see you again?" He kept throwing questions out there but she ignored them all.

She looked around the room, clearly missing something. I spotted it first. Her phone was sitting on the nightstand on my side of the bed. I grabbed it before she saw it. She couldn't leave if she didn't have her phone. Was it a juvenile move? Maybe. But I was desperate and willing to do whatever it took to buy us more time. "You don't have to talk to us now, sweets. But you can't expect us to just leave town. To leave you. Not after last night."

I watched her take a deep breath as she glared at me, her

gaze dropping to her phone like she could will it out of my hands. "You promised one night."

Her voice sounded husky and choked, like she was on the verge of tears. What the hell? I was about to ask her what she was keeping from us when her phone dinged. I looked down at it in my hands, lit up with a text. I didn't read the message, my attention was too focused on the picture in the background.

I muttered a curse under my breath as I studied the picture of Ivy with her arms wrapped around a little girl. A girl who was the spitting image of Ivy. Rory snatched the phone out of my hands to see what I was staring at as I looked up at Ivy.

I felt as if I'd been kicked in the gut. This—no, *she*—was why Ivy was running?

Her eyes were wide and her lips parted like she might say something, but no words came out.

"Holy shit." Rory handed the phone back to me like I might know what to do with this new information. "Is that your daughter?"

Of course it was her fucking daughter, but we had to get confirmation. Had to know for certain.

She paused for a second before nodding. The girl looked just like her and we both knew Ivy had no siblings so it couldn't have been a niece or nephew. Which only left a daughter.

Holy shit, Ivy was a mom.

"Who's the father?" I asked. Suspicion gave my tone a hard edge and I saw her blink rapidly in response. This was exactly what I'd feared. There was no way in hell Ivy was single—I should have known that was why she had been so hesitant to see us, why she was running out now.

Rory rubbed his face like he was trying to wake himself up from a dream. "Are you involved with someone, Ivy?" His voice was kinder than mine had been and some of her shock seemed to fade.

"I told you I wasn't," she whispered. It was almost hard to hear her words over the hum of the air conditioning.

Rory gave me a look that made me feel guilty for jumping to conclusions. She hadn't been having an affair with us. Thank god.

"So who was he?" I asked, swinging my feet over the side of the bed, grabbing my boxers off the floor and slipping them on. I didn't want to talk about a guy who got her pregnant with my dick hanging out. "Did you get married? Were you in a relationship in college?"

Ivy's brow creased in confusion as she looked from me to Rory. Then she shook her head and sighed. "God, you guys don't even see it."

Rory and I looked at each other. "See what?" I asked.

Ivy bit her lip and looked up toward the ceiling. Then she exhaled loudly and faced us. "That's my daughter, Lily. She's six years old."

Rory and I were silent as that sank in.

After a second, Ivy groaned. "You guys have never been good with math, have you? She's yours, boys. Lily was conceived that night in Baker's field."

The silence was deafening as Rory and I stared at Ivy. I had a daughter...or Rory had a daughter. Either way...*we* had a daughter.

For the second time in my life, my world flipped upside down. But unlike the accident, this upheaval didn't make me crash and burn. It lifted me up, opening a space in my chest I didn't even know was there.

Holy shit, we had a kid. A daughter. *Lily.*

I looked to Rory and saw that he was just as awed by this revelation. We had a kid. A kid that we'd never known about. A kid who probably didn't know we existed. A jolt of anger had me jumping out of bed and reaching for my jeans. "Why didn't you tell us?"

She crossed her arms in front of her chest. "I had my reasons." Ivy had never been good at lying or being evasive. Every one of her emotions showed on her face and right now I could see the fear, the guilt, the regrets plain as day. She might have had her reasons, but she was far from confident about her actions.

Rory was out of bed now too, halfway dressed as he crossed over to her. I could see the pent-up anger in his body and understood it. To Rory, family was everything. He'd never had one to speak of—not one that was loving anyhow. And all he'd ever wanted was for us to have the family he'd never had. We'd come here to make that, not discover we'd been lied to, to be denied what he'd wanted all along.

"You should have told us, Ivy. We could have—"

"What?" she snapped. "You could have what? Put your dreams on hold? Given up a chance for a career in the military so you could stay in Bridgewater and raise a baby at eighteen? You could have supported us with that part-time job you had to get at the grocery store to pay for diapers?"

Her eyes flashed with anger, but it was a defensive anger. Still, her point hit home. I turned to Rory. "What the hell could we have done back then?"

He shrugged, clearly irritated that I wasn't on his side. "I don't know. But we would have helped. We would have stepped up." He ran a hand through his short hair. "Hell, we would have loved her."

Ivy's eyes were suspiciously bright, like she was fighting

back tears. "I know you would have, Rory." She looked at me. "And you, too. I knew you both would do the right thing if I'd told you. Which was exactly why I didn't."

She dropped her arms and let out a sigh. "I didn't want to make you guys feel trapped or think you needed to put your lives on hold. We were too young, we were all too young."

I could see that Rory wanted to argue, but he let her speak.

"By the time I found out, you boys were off at boot camp and I was in Seattle." She shrugged as if at a loss for words. "I had to make some tough decisions, and I had to make them on my own. Besides, it wasn't as if the army would understand the Bridgewater lifestyle. They wouldn't let *both* of you just leave because you said you'd fucked me together and wanted to do the right thing."

She looked so bereft as she stared down at her feet, I moved toward her on instinct and pulled her into my arms, into a tight hold.

"I'm sorry," she said softly as she leaned into my embrace. "I'm so sorry."

I looked over at Rory and saw that some of his anger had drained away, most likely at the realization that she'd been right. We hadn't been in a place to help her. And whether we liked it or not, she'd been in a tough position and had been forced to make difficult choices. I didn't care if Lily was actually mine or Rory's. A Bridgewater child belonged to both fathers, regardless of DNA. The government wouldn't have seen it that way, but that didn't matter.

We might still have our issues with Ivy and the way she'd handled things back then, but there was one thing I was clear on. One thing I knew without asking that Rory would agree with.

I pushed Ivy back slightly so I could look down into her tear-filled blue eyes. "We need to see her, Ivy. We want to meet our daughter. We aren't eighteen anymore heading off to boot camp. We're back for good. We're with you—and Lily—for good."

7

Cooper drove, Ivy sitting up front beside him so we didn't get lost in the endless maze of cul-de-sacs and tree lined streets in her picturesque Seattle suburb.

My foot kept bouncing as we drew further and further into the labyrinth of ranch-style homes and closer and closer to our daughter.

Our daughter.

Since the rental car was short on leg room, my knee kept hitting the back of Cooper's seat.

"Would you quit it? You're making me nervous," Cooper said.

"Then join the club," I muttered. I wasn't too macho to admit that I was nervous. Hell, I was scared shitless. *We had a fucking daughter.* The phrase had been repeating on a loop since the moment we found out. It was like my brain thought that if it repeated the phrase enough, it would suddenly register and make sense.

It wasn't working. No amount of repetition would make this feel real. Maybe once we saw her—Lily— I could wrap my head around it. But seeing her was what made me want to take a nose dive out of this moving car.

I didn't know many kids. I never had siblings growing up and I didn't have any friends with little ones now. The army didn't cater to children. I didn't even know how to interact with a random child, let alone a girl who was either my daughter by blood or my daughter by adoption. Either way, she was mine, and now that I knew she even existed, there was no way in hell I was letting her go.

Some residual anger threatened to overwhelm me, but I pushed it aside. I might not like the choices that Ivy made back then, but when she gave us some time alone to talk while she took a shower in our hotel room—no fucking way were we letting her leave without us—Cooper helped me to see just how scared she must have been back then.

Eighteen and pregnant. Alone. Her grandmother had died soon after we left. She'd given up college, at least for a few years. She'd only had her aunt for support.

It was easy to say now that she'd made the wrong choice by not getting in touch with us, but there was no way we could put ourselves in that position. We were guys and never had to think about it, but fuck. What would I have done in a similar situation? Would I have held her back from her dream of college and a teaching career?

Logically, I knew I couldn't judge. Still, logic wasn't exactly ruling the roost at the moment. I looked at the back of her blonde head, saw the way she kept her chin up when her world had changed with our arrival. It showed me how brave she was. Fuck, she'd always been brave. I was going to face a six-year-old and I was ready to hurl. Rocket propelled grenades I could handle, but a child I'd made? I swallowed hard.

"Do you think she'll like us?" I asked.

Stupid question, but I couldn't help myself. Cooper gave a noncommittal shrug. He'd been getting quieter and surlier as we drove. I had no idea what was going on in that head of his, but I had a feeling it wasn't good. He hadn't had a nightmare with Ivy in his arms, thank fuck, but I had to hope seeing Lily wouldn't put him in a tailspin. Ivy's silence was even more disturbing. Was she as afraid of us meeting Lily as we were? Did she think Lily wouldn't like us?

Before I could ask any more stupid questions, Ivy told Cooper to park on the street in front of her house. It had been dark out when we'd picked her up the night before and now I could take in the picture-perfect setting. It was a white house, two-story with black trim and red front door. The street was tree-lined and every lawn was neatly cut with perfectly pruned hedges. A child's bike was casually left out on the neighbor's front yard indicating families lived here. This wasn't just a house, but a home. A home with a six-year-old. "Looks like you've done well for yourself, sweets."

I didn't mean for it to sound like an accusation, but some of the resentment and anger from earlier had slipped into my voice, making the simple statement sound churlish. Shit. I ran my hand over my face with regret, but didn't apologize.

It was no wonder she responded in a defensive tone and only flicked me with her gaze before looking away. "It's my great aunt's house. When I found out I was pregnant, Aunt Sarah asked me to move in with her. Since my grandma had just passed, I had nowhere else to go."

Fuck. I was such an ass and the way Cooper looked over his shoulder at me, he agreed. If we weren't about to meet our daughter, he'd probably punch me in the face.

Rationally, I knew she didn't have to justify herself to me, but I wanted to understand. I needed to know everything that had happened back then. She'd told us *why* she hadn't come to us, but she'd never said what made her think we wouldn't be good for Lily. She was six, plenty of time for her to let us know, and if we hadn't shown up out of the blue, I doubted she would have ever told us. We never would have known our little girl looked just like her mother. "You could have come to us." I'd said it before, but I felt like I had to say it again, to let her know we wouldn't have abandoned her.

I heard her sigh as she opened her door. Cooper climbed out of the car and went around to her and I followed suit. She didn't look at me as she led the way up the path to her porch. Halfway there, she spun on her heel and surprised me. "Maybe you're right." She looked me in the eye, lifted her chin. From her perch on the step, she was almost at eye level and her lips were pressed into a thin line. For the first time, I realized just how hard this must be for her, too. "Maybe that's what I should have done."

But she hadn't. That part went unsaid, but her point was clear. Whether it was right or wrong, it was done. I glanced up at the door we were rapidly approaching and those goddamn nerves threatened to eat me alive.

"If you guys could just—" She shoved a lock of hair back behind her ear and let out a long exhale. "If you could just let me do the talking, that would be great."

I looked to Cooper and knew what he was thinking. No problem. Neither of us knew what to say to this kid. *Our* kid.

As far as I was concerned, Ivy could run this show until I wasn't scared so shitless.

We heard Lily before we saw her as we stepped inside the house. A TV was on in a room nearby and whatever was happening on the screen made her laugh. I came to a stop as sweet little girl laughter hit us. I looked over at Cooper and saw that he looked just as shocked as I felt. Like a two-by-four struck me in the back of the head. Hearing her laugh made it all so real. *She* was real, not just a picture in a phone.

Now that we were inside, Ivy seemed determined to get this over with. She didn't stop to give us time to adjust, just walked straight into the living room and we followed behind her.

I'd seen the picture, but it didn't do Lily justice.

Fuck me.

She was stunning. A little angel, with her mama's blonde hair and blue eyes. And those eyes were fixed on Cooper and me, studying us with curiosity. I was vaguely aware of another person in the room but it wasn't until she stepped into my line of sight that I really noticed her.

"You must be Rory and Cooper," the gray-haired woman said with a smile.

Not only was I scared of a child, but I'd forgotten all my manners.

Ivy made the introductions. "Rory, Cooper, this is my great aunt, Sarah. I told her you were coming." Judging by the knowing look the older woman gave us, Ivy had also told her what our relationship was to Lily. The fact that we were dropping her niece off at ten in the morning instead of last night, she probably had a pretty good idea what we'd been up to.

"Nice to meet you, ma'am," Cooper said. I looked over

and saw that he was still staring at the little girl, apparently just as fascinated as I was at the sight of her.

"Lily, honey," Ivy said. "Come on over here and meet my...my friends."

I shot her a look. Friends? So that's how she wanted to spin this. We were just some random friends dropping by to say hello?

My original anger was back, but I swallowed it down as Lily climbed off the couch and headed our way. Coming to a stop next to Ivy, she pressed herself up against her mother's leg as she gave us a shy smile. She wore a bright pink nightgown that fell to her ankles, her blonde locks slightly tangled from sleep. "Hello."

Without thinking, I dropped down to her level and reached out a hand. "Pleasure to meet you, Lily. I'm Rory."

Her answering smile was magic, just like her mother's. Then she turned her gaze up to Cooper. I saw him freeze as she reached out to touch his hand. It was his bad arm, the one that was covered in scars, although they were hidden by the long sleeve of his shirt. A flurry of emotions—dark and jagged—chased across his face as he stared at her and her tiny, outstretched hand. Mumbling something I couldn't understand, he turned tail and bolted, his footfall heavy on the wood floor, the screen door slapping loudly behind him. Instinctively, I stood to go after him but Ivy stopped me with a shake of her head.

"No," she said. "Let me go."

I nodded. She was right. I'd been trying to help him for months, but what he really needed right now was Ivy. And Lily. He needed our family. He knew I was his best friend and I was always there for him, but he was tired of hearing the same-old from me, that it hadn't been his fault. He hadn't been responsible for all those lives, all of those men who'd died when his chopper had been hit by the fucking RPG. He'd been able to keep the bird in the air long enough so the crash happened where a rescue team could get to him, to bring all the men's bodies home to be buried. He was a fucking hero, but he didn't see it that way.

And now, out of the blue, he had a kid. A kid who would look to him to stay safe. Whole. Healthy. I couldn't help him with this because I was freaking the fuck out too. A little girl with blond ringlets and blue eyes looked up at me—her head tilted way back because I was so much bigger—with something like awe and unconditional trust. Her little head cocked to the side and I recognized the same gesture in her mother.

My love for Ivy had grown over time. My love for Lily, instantaneous.

Just like that, my mind was made up. Ivy might have had her reasons for doing what she had, but things were different now. We were here and we weren't going anywhere. Whether Ivy wanted us or not, nothing would change the fact that Lily was ours, too. Yeah, we might have a fledgling business started in Bridgewater, but we had a daughter. She came first. Seattle, Bridgewater, I didn't give a fuck. I wasn't missing another minute with her.

Hopefully, we'd all be a family soon enough, a unit, but even if we couldn't win Ivy over, there was no way I would ever walk away from this girl, not now that she was in our lives.

I dropped to my knees again, leaned back on my heels so we were eye to eye.

"That man, he's scared," she said, her voice soft and gentle.

Perceptive little thing. She got her smarts from Ivy, that was for sure.

I darted a glance at Aunt Sarah, who gave a slight nod along with a small, reassuring smile.

"He is." I cleared my throat.

"Of me?"

When Lily looked at me with those big eyes filled with worry, I told her what she needed to know.

8

*I*VY

I found Cooper on the back porch, leaning over the railing as though he might be sick. I hesitated for a moment before coming up close and wrapping my arms around his waist. I felt the heat of him through his shirt. He stiffened for just a second before relaxing against me. He was so different now than the night before. Then, he'd been all heat and passion, dominance and focus. Now? Vulnerable. Fearful.

"Are you all right?" I asked, keeping my voice soft.

He turned around to face me and leaned a hip against the rail. The truth of it was there in his eyes. No, he wasn't all right. It had been a stupid question and I didn't want to make him say it aloud. So I asked another. "Why did you walk out?"

His expression was so pained, it almost hurt to look at him.

"I didn't want to scare her." His voice was deep, cracked.

I blinked up at him in surprise. That thought had never even occurred to me. He might be big and brawny, but he was the most gentle person I knew. Besides Rory. "Scare her? How on earth could you scare her?"

He drew in a deep breath and shrugged, looked down at the porch floor. "I don't know...my scars, my nightmares." He lifted his head, met my gaze. "Ivy, there have been days I can barely drag myself out of bed without Rory prodding me. I'm not the same guy I was before."

"No, you're not," I agreed, crossing my arms over my chest so I didn't reach out and comfort him. That wasn't what he needed right now. There was no use denying he wasn't eighteen anymore. His gaze held experience. Hardship. Tragedy. But that meant he had lived, and survived.

The other day, the difference in him had been obvious. He no longer had that easy, open attitude. He was guarded, pained, and maybe rightfully so. He did a good job to hide it, but I knew him too well.

"You're stronger than you were before," I told him, opting to focus on the positive changes I'd seen. And he *was* stronger. He might not have that youthful charm anymore, but he held himself with a kind of poise and strength that only came with maturity and life experience.

He turned his face to look out at our backyard where Lily's swing set sat surrounded by a boatload of toys. "I don't know if I should be around children."

I gave a little snort of amusement at that. When he looked over in surprise, I explained. "Lily isn't 'children.' She's not just some random kid. She's your child. Of course you should be around her."

His gaze focused on my face, as if trying to read something there. As if I might be lying. I wasn't. I trusted him, perhaps more than he trusted himself. But now that I'd made the decision to introduce them to Lily, I had no doubts she would love them just like I always had. She was perceptive. All children were. She would see Cooper for what he was. Good, inside and out.

With that in mind, I took a step closer to him and took his hand in mine. "She's your daughter," I said again. "Which means she's strong, just like you. Trust me, she can handle some scars and some moodiness. Just wait until she's thirteen. She'll give your moodiness a run for the money."

One side of his mouth curved up in amusement at my description. I tugged on his hand, forcing him to follow me. "Come on. It's time you said hello to your daughter. I promise she'll love you."

We no sooner stepped into the living room than Lily ran over to me, her nightgown swirling around her ankles, her face lit up with excitement. "Is it true, Mommy? Are these my daddies?"

Shock left me temporarily speechless. I shot a look at Rory who came into the room behind her. He watched us with his arms crossed defensively. He'd told her and he was ready for my anger. I'd wanted to tell Lily in my own way, my own time, but he'd taken that from me. They both had when they showed up the other day out of the blue.

And though I was angry that he'd gone ahead and spilled the news first, I'd have been lying if I said I wasn't just a little bit relieved. I'd been dreading how I was going to tell her, especially since I'd kept it a secret until now, but she knew and she was...well, she was over the moon.

Lily questioned everything, just like every other curious

child. *Why is the moon white? Where do rabbits go at night? Why is broccoli green and not pink?* But those were easy to answer. And the question she asked now? It was easy to answer as well.

"It's true, sweetheart. These men are your daddies." I saw Aunt Sarah come to stand beside Rory, her eyes filled with tears. She'd always wanted me to introduce Lily to her fathers and she'd finally gotten her wish.

Lily ran over to Cooper and wrapped her arms around his waist. Rory and I watched as Cooper—tough, guarded, broken Cooper—got tears in his eyes looking down at his little girl. Carefully, he put his hands on her back, patted it gently. I knew without a doubt that Lily, with her unconditional love, was exactly what Cooper needed in his life to help him heal. It wasn't going to be immediate, but we had nothing but time now. As if on cue, Lily spotted the scar that crept out from beneath his sleeve and covered part of his hand. She pulled back, her eyes wide with excitement. "I have a booboo, too!" She proudly pulled up the sleeve of her nightgown to show him where she'd cut herself the other day on the jungle gym.

Cooper blinked down at her, clearly stunned, but she was oblivious to his shock. "See?" she said. "We match."

He nodded. "Yeah, I see." Wrapping an arm around her shoulders, he held her tight and I had to turn away to keep from outright bawling. I'd kept her from these men, from this joy that was immediate for her. I'd kept Cooper and Rory from their daughter, from this perfect connection which they shared, even after knowing each other a few minutes.

The rest of the day passed by in a blur of emotions. I mostly sat back and watched in awe as Lily played and chatted with the guys as if it was the most natural thing in the world. And those men—my men—they were surprisingly good with her. For a couple of badass war heroes who said they were afraid of a child, they knew their way around a Barbie playhouse and seemed to have no qualms about partaking some imaginary tea alongside her stuffed animal collection.

I watched as Aunt Sarah stifled a laugh when Cooper sat in a little chair meant for someone Lily's size, his knees almost in his nose. I couldn't hold it back and Cooper glanced up at me, grinned. He was so handsome. Seeing this softer side of him only made me want him more.

When dinnertime rolled around, Rory went out onto the porch and showed Lily his special trick for grilling the perfect burger. I was emotionally exhausted by the time I put her down to bed shortly after dinner.

Luckily Lily went down easily—no doubt she was just as exhausted as I was. She handled it well, but both of our lives had been flipped upside down and there was no going back to the way it was.

What that meant for how we moved forward, though... well, that remained to be seen. When I came back downstairs, Aunt Sarah graciously excused herself saying she had an important bridge game down at the senior center and slipped out the front door, pocketbook slung over her arm and a smirk on her lips. She was even brash enough to wink at the men.

While it *was* Bridge night, I knew very well that she was trying to give us some space for a much needed talk. This wasn't just a one-night-stand anymore. She wasn't telling me to have a good time with two hot cowboys as she had—at least subtly—the night before. This was different. This was more. This was everything.

Judging by the curious looks she'd been giving me all day, I'd have plenty of explaining to do when she and I had a moment alone. I hadn't told her who my date was the night before. I'd given her no notice when we showed up this morning, not that I'd had any either. She'd always known about Rory and Cooper—I hadn't kept it from her—but neither of us knew about what they'd endured in the military and how seeing Lily would impact them. Would impact all of us. But first and foremost, I had to figure out what the hell was going on. Cooper wasn't freaking because he just discovered he had a child. No, he freaked because he didn't think he was *good* enough for her. That he'd hurt her. Scare her. They knew my secret and it was time to learn theirs.

Cooper sat quietly on the couch as Rory scowled from where he leaned against the doorframe. Clearly, he'd been waiting for me, and judging by his look, he was waiting for a fight.

"You had no right to tell her you were her fathers," I said, turning to face him.

His eyes darkened, his square jaw clenched. It was exactly what he'd been waiting for. Pushing himself off the doorframe, he walked toward me. Being so big, his footsteps were almost silent. "I had every right. She's our daughter, Ivy. She deserves to know that, just like we deserved to know when she was born."

I looked away, my shoulders slumping, all bluster gone because he was right. I was angry for the upheaval, the confusion. I'd been doing things my way all along, being the one in charge, making the important decisions. Alone. Now they showed up out of nowhere and stake their claim. Over me, their daughter. It was too much, too fast.

"I know," I said. And I did. But that didn't make it any

easier, or any less overwhelming. I tried to explain it to them. "I was planning on telling Lily eventually. I just wanted some time to figure out how this will work. You showed up two days ago!" I saw my men exchange a look and hurried on. "I know you want to be a part of her life, but we don't know what that will look like yet. You'll be going back to Bridgewater and we'll be here and...I just don't want to see her disappointed."

Rory sighed as he crossed the distance between us. "Sweets, do you really think we could ever walk away from you or Lily? Hell, we weren't planning on leaving here without you, but now knowing what we do about Lily... there's no way we're letting you go. Either of you."

I shook my head. This was all happening too quickly. I took a step back.

"We'll stay here in Seattle if that's what it takes," Cooper said quietly.

I looked from him to Rory who nodded in agreement.

"No way. I couldn't ask you to do that. You have a new business and a home of your own and—"

"Then come back with us," Rory interrupted. He reached out and tucked my hair behind my ear. It seemed he liked to do that, to touch my hair, to see my face. They'd told me long ago they could see every one of my emotions on my face. Perhaps it was true, because he was looking at me so intently, so deeply. "Bring Lily to Bridgewater."

I opened my mouth but was too stunned to say anything. What they were asking was ludicrous. "Montana? We have a life here. A good one."

Rory shrugged as if the issue wasn't huge. "Then we'll stay here."

My eyes widened at his casual promise. Like it was a

given they would drop everything and move to Seattle for us.

Cooper spoke up again. "You've got to understand that you and Lily are the most important things to us. More important than any business or house. Those are *things*. We learned in the army that people matter. They're irreplaceable. We have you. We have a child. Jesus, we have a daughter and we won't miss a minute more of her."

"All that matters is that we're in your lives," Rory added. "However you'll have us."

The last of my energy drained out of me at those words. It was too much, too soon. I had no idea how to respond. I felt like I could sleep for days—I'd been kept up late by their thorough attentions the night before—and maybe then meditate for a year, and after that maybe I'd know what the right thing to do was. But for now, my brain was fried and my heart was filled to the brim with too many emotions to name. "Can we...can we talk about this tomorrow? I'm not saying no," I clarified. "I need some time."

Rory's answering grin was wicked. A look I remembered from high school that had me handing over my panties, and my virginity. "I think we could all use a break right about now." He reached out and pulled me into his arms. I didn't resist. I didn't want to. "Let us help you relax."

I was already breathless and melting in his arms when he murmured, "What do you say?"

I heard Cooper move behind me, pressing his front against my back. They liked me between them as much as I liked being there. I felt secure, safe. Protected. As if they could block out the world with their large bodies.

What did I say? Yes. Hell, yes.

I might not know what to do about them and Lily, but I knew what we had was spectacular. Special. I couldn't deny it. I couldn't argue because I would be lying and they'd know. My orgasms from the night before were proof enough. Rory couldn't miss my hard nipples pressing into his chest. I wanted them. I ached for them and I couldn't deny any of us the pleasure we could share.

Cooper said people mattered. Rory and Cooper mattered to me. What was between us—even with how confusing it was—mattered.

I tipped my head toward my bedroom in the back of the house on the main floor. "My room is that way."

Cooper stepped back and Rory scooped me up into his arms so quickly I let out a little squeal. When he set me on my feet by my bed, Cooper was there to greet me with a kiss that made me forget all about the major life decisions I had yet to face. The heat of it, the feel of his lips on mine made me whimper. When he used that to his advantage and his tongue slipped in to meet mine, I met him with a burst of need. I put my hands on him, slid them down his muscular torso to the bottom of his shirt, pushed it up. Felt the heat of his skin beneath.

Rory's hands moved beneath the skirt of my sundress I'd changed into earlier in the day. He grunted when he felt my bare butt, then the lacy string of my thong. In one quick move, he tugged them down so they fell to my ankles. I heard his voice in my ear as Cooper's tongue slid against mine. "I can't wait, sweets. This is going to be fast, at least the first time. Bend over."

Oh my. That growled command was enough to make me wet—no, wetter—and I let him and Cooper maneuver me over the bed so I was resting on my forearms, my bare ass in the air. They were quiet and I glanced over my shoulder. Standing side by side, they were looking at my butt. And my pussy. Rory stroked a hand over my hip, then slipped his fingers through my wetness. I arched my back and cried out at the barely-there caress.

"Fuck," he murmured. "Fast, sweets. We're going to take you fast."

I wiggled my hips. "Yes," I breathed, wanton and eager for them.

I watched as they unfastened their jeans, pulled their cocks out.

Cooper's hands gripped my hips to hold me still. "Easy. You know we'll always take care of you. But first you need to learn your lesson."

I was almost ashamed to say how much those words turned me on. I'd never thought I was into power plays in the bedroom, but this was a side of the boys—no, *men*—that made my pussy ache. "What lesson?" I managed to ask, my voice breathless with anticipation. "What happened to fast?"

"Don't worry, that's coming," Rory said. "But Cooper's right. You should have let us take care of you back then and every day since."

His hand came down on my ass with a loud slap. I let out a little cry and bit my lip as the sting from his palm turned into something deliciously hot. They'd never spanked me before. Hell, I'd never been spanked by any man before and it was hot. I never imagined I'd like it, the feel of Rory's palm making contact with my upturned bottom. That he was taking charge, turning his words, his feelings into something I could physically feel.

"It's our job to take care of you," Cooper said as he spanked me next. I moaned and arched my back, lifting my ass higher and silently begging for more.

"Your problems are ours. You're our woman and your happiness means everything to us." Rory spanked me hard, making me jerk forward with a gasp.

"Rory!"

"Do you understand?" Cooper asked as he grabbed my hips and pulled me back into position. Oh my god, I didn't know this side of them, this dominance was...exhilarating.

"Yes," I gasped. I bit my lip, but couldn't stop myself from adding, "I want more."

Rory's laugh was low and pleased as he stroked his palm over my heated skin. "Our naughty girl likes her punishment. We'll give you what you need, but first you will promise to let us help you from here on out. Whatever you need, we're here for you."

I nodded quickly, his words making me tear up with a tenderness that was almost unbearable. It seemed crazy since I was on my hands and knees, dress tossed up about my waist. There were no doubt handprints—their big ones —on my bottom. And I wanted more. I wanted anything they'd give me. I'd been on my own for so long I'd almost forgotten what it felt like to be taken care of. To be loved. And hopefully in the next few seconds, well and truly fucked. "I promise."

"Good girl." Then he gave me what I craved—another hard spanking that had me pleading incoherently for more. Shit, I was so turned on I was barely making sense. Was it possible to come from a spanking?

Cooper moved around the bed, dropped onto it so his head was propped up on my pile of decorative pillows and tugged me forward and on top of him. He'd opened his pants and his cock stood up straight. The vein along the thick length pulsed. The sight of it made my mouth water. I flicked my gaze to his, then grinned. Lowering my head, I opened my mouth to suck his cock, but he had other ideas. Handing me a condom wrapper, I opened it and rolled it down his hard length, his fists clenched in my comforter as

I did so. Once sheathed, he pulled me up easily with his rock-hard physique. I would have to remember to send a thank you note to Uncle Sam for all the extra muscles my man had packed on. I was straddling him, my knees on either side of his narrow hips and he helped me lower myself on top of him, his hard length sliding into me and filling me up.

I rolled my hips, grinding against him, adjusting to him. He was so big, so deep I was desperate for release, especially after that spanking. I felt Rory behind me, grab the hem of my dress and tug it up. I lifted my arms over my head and he worked the dress off, my bare breasts bouncing free. His hands cupped them as I rode his friend. His fingers pinched my nipples hard and my head fell back against his shoulder. Yes. This. This was what I'd been missing all these years. The heady, mindless joy of being fucked by two men whose sole mission was to make me happy, to take care of me and fulfill my desires.

Who could ever walk away from this?

Me. I'd walked away from it once but it had nearly killed me. I honestly didn't know if I could ever do it again.

"Come, sweets," Rory breathed, licking along the delicate shell of my ear. One hand slid down and over my clit, slick and hard, pushing me over the edge.

I rode Cooper's cock as I came, sweat blooming on my skin. Only when the pleasure ebbed did they move.

"Ready for us both?" Rory asked, moving back to put a condom on. I heard the pop of a lid, the slick squirt of liquid.

I jolted when Rory's palm cupped my bottom, then slid a finger over my back entrance. Cooper gripped my hips, tugged me down so I was laying on his chest. His pale eyes met mine. "Let Rory fuck your ass. Take us together."

My eyes widened when I felt Rory's finger pressing against me more insistently. There.

"Ever had a cock here before?" he asked.

I shook my head and shuddered as he circled, pressed in.

"Oh god," I moaned. I'd had no idea I was so sensitive from such an intimate touch. I clenched down on Cooper's cock, making him groan.

"Shit, woman. You're squeezing my dick and I'm going to come. Let Rory take this virginity, too. I love knowing we'll always be your firsts."

Rory continued to play as Cooper continued. I breathed deeply, trying to remain relaxed as Rory worked to carefully stretch me open, to become used to being doubly filled. "I want Rory inside you when I come, when we'll make you come again. All three of us. Together."

He wasn't one of many words, but he wanted this. The way Rory was coaxing me, with a gentleness that surprised me, into my virgin asshole, I had to admit I kind of wanted it, too.

I knew this was the kind of sex people in threesomes had, that it was common in Bridgewater—I might have been a virgin until right before I left for college, but I hadn't been that naive—but had never tried it myself. I'd only had Rory and Cooper for one night.

Cooper nudged his hips up, rubbing deep inside, breaking me from my thoughts.

"Yes!" I cried, allowing them to do what they wanted. What *I* wanted.

Rory gently pushed a finger into me deeper and deeper, slick and coated with lube.

"Easy," I breathed, telling Rory what I liked, what I needed. "Slow."

I watched Cooper as Rory worked me, adding more and more lube to ease his way. I heard the squirt again, heard as he coated his condom-covered cock.

His large body came up over me, a hand resting beside my head, beside Cooper's shoulder. I felt the hard lines of his chest against my back.

"That's right. Nice and slow and easy," Rory murmured. I felt the broad head press against me, even while Cooper filled my pussy.

"That's it, sweets. Good girl. Let me in. Let us fuck you together for the first time. You're what brings us together."

Rory continued to talk. Dirty things, sweet things, gentling sounds as I opened more and more for him until with a silent pop, he was in. I cried out at the fullness of it.

Cooper stroked my hair, leaned up to kiss me, to swallow the sounds of me finally taking both my men at the same time.

The sensation was new—a little painful and a whole lot overwhelming—but Rory was gentle as he teased my asshole open for his cock. It might have hurt if I hadn't been so relaxed from them getting me off first. I was wet for Cooper and Rory had made sure I was well lubed for him. Cooper began to slowly move, carefully pulling back just a bit and sliding in as Rory slid in deeper and deeper. He reached around and with his fingers, teased my clit. Soon they were both fully inside me and holy shit, I had no words.

I was so full, so complete. Open. Exposed. Vulnerable, but they'd protect me. Keep me safe. Make me feel so damn good. They rode me hard, filling me up over and over until I couldn't hold back the cry of pleasure. I clenched and squeezed them, milked their cocks until they came, too. I silently wished there was no barrier between us, that they'd give me their seed. I wanted to take it deep until I was marked, body and soul. My head rested on Cooper's sweaty chest and I listened as his heartbeat slowed. Rory slid from me, went to the bathroom and returned. Only then did Cooper pull out so they could clean me up, then settle me between them. Right where I belonged. I fell asleep wrapped in their arms. Sore, yet satisfied.

9

*I*VY

I awoke at dawn, but they were gone, their spots on either side of me cold. My body felt well used, a lingering soreness that had me smiling. I never imagined I'd take them together. Perhaps sucking on one of their cocks while the other fucked me, but not with both of them deep inside me, pussy and ass.

Okay, maybe I had, but reality? It was more amazing than I'd ever imagined.

I hadn't heard when they'd left, but I knew they weren't running away as I'd planned to do the morning before. I knew they'd intentionally left before Aunt Sarah and Lily awoke. They might have been quick to spread the news that they were Lily's fathers, but none of us was eager to explain what Mommy's friends were doing having a sleepover in her bedroom. I was thankful for the courtesy and respect.

Breakfast was just me, Lily, and Aunt Sarah again, as it

had always been, but if felt different. Funny how after just one day I found this threesome to be entirely lacking. Cooper and Rory had somehow managed to make themselves indispensable and I wasn't the only one who seemed to feel that way. Usually a chatterbox in the morning, it was all I could do to get Lily to talk about anything else but her newfound fathers.

After breakfast, I sent her off to play in her room while I cleaned up the kitchen. I wasn't surprised when Aunt Sarah lingered, her knowing gaze fixed on me as I made a show of clearing the table.

"Well?" she asked. While I had on a pair of old pajama pants and a t-shirt, she was dressed in crisp capri pants and a red pullover. Her white hair was neat and tidy.

"Well, what?" I countered, putting the syrup bottle back in the cabinet.

She arched her brows and peered at me over the rim of her glasses. "Don't play dumb, dear. It doesn't suit you."

I let out a snort of amusement. "Sorry I didn't give you more of a heads up about their coming yesterday. Their reappearance came as a bit of a shock."

She nodded. "I suspected as much. So, how are you feeling about their new involvement in your life?"

I lingered over scrubbing the frying pan to avoid her penetrating gaze. How did I feel? That was a loaded question. Sore between my thighs, but I wasn't going to tell her that, and that certainly wasn't what she meant. It had all happened so quickly, I'd barely had time to process. One minute they were surprising the hell out of me in the school parking lot and the next they were announcing to Lily the fact that they were her fathers. Then I was taking them both at the same time. How was I supposed to feel about that? How was I supposed to *explain* that to my daughter when none of her little friends had two daddies?

Aunt Sarah laughed softly behind me. "I wasn't trying to stump you with that question."

I stopped scrubbing long enough to meet her amused gaze. I managed a small smile in return. "Sorry, I guess I haven't sorted that out yet."

"That's what too much kissing can do."

I rolled my eyes and couldn't help the way my cheeks heated.

My aunt crossed her arms. "You're trying to use your brain to figure out an issue of the heart."

I flipped the pot over in the drying rack and nodded. Maybe she was right. "Maybe I am overthinking things. But Lily's involved, and if this doesn't go well, she could get hurt. I can't just act on a whim when her happiness is at stake."

"There you go, overthinking again," Aunt Sarah pointed out. "What does your heart say?"

I groaned as I dropped the pretense that I was still cleaning and leaned against the counter. What did my heart say? That was easy. My heart wanted to be with them. My heart had said *mine* the moment I saw them in the parking lot. I'd never felt anything close to the connection I felt with them and I knew I never would.

They might be Bridgewater men, but I was also born and raised in the Bridgewater way and there was no doubt in my mind that those two were mine, just like I was theirs. "My heart says that we should give this a shot," I started. "But what if it doesn't work out? What if Lily gets hurt? And how would this even work? I have a home here in Seattle and they've started a life for themselves in Bridgewater."

"One thing at a time, dear," Aunt Sarah said. Her eyes were lit up with laughter as she studied me. She'd never married, but I didn't doubt her sage advice. "What did those fine young men say? What do they want?"

My chest tightened at the memory of Rory's words. *All that matters is that we're in your lives. However you'll have us.*

"They said they'd move to Seattle, if that's what I wanted," I replied. I picked up the dishtowel, folded it, then put it on the counter. "Or they invited us to Bridgewater." I shrugged. "All that matters to them is that they're in Lily's life."

"And yours, I imagine," Aunt Sarah said.

And in my bed.

"Don't think I didn't see the way they were watching you." She let out a low whistle. "My goodness, girl. I nearly melted on the spot with those looks they were giving."

I struggled to hold back a laugh. "I don't know what you're talking about."

"Mmm-hmm." Her laugh was downright wicked. "Take it from an old lady—that kind of passion doesn't last forever. If you ask me, you should take full advantage."

My face was burning as I grabbed up the folded dishtowel and made a show of wiping down the table so I wouldn't have to face her. Aunt Sarah had never been what anyone would call traditional, but there was no way in hell I could talk to her about my current sex life with Rory and Cooper. *Especially* the way we'd heated up the sheets the night before. I was just glad Lily was a heavy sleeper and Aunt Sarah hadn't been home when they'd taken me together. Cooper's kisses had barely stifled my sounds of pleasure as I came.

Aunt Sarah seemed to get the hint and she steered the topic away from those hot looks...and more. "I think you should go to Bridgewater."

I shot up straight and turned to face her. "You do? But

Seattle is our home. It's the only home Lily has ever known, she—"

She held up a hand to stop me. "I'm not saying you've got to move there right away. I just think you owe it to yourself to go back to your hometown." She took a step closer to me and gently took the rag from my hand. "Honey, you haven't been back since your grandma died and, while I understand why, you have no reason to stay away anymore. It's summer vacation. Go. Have some fun."

The truth of her statement struck me dumb. It was true, the main reason I never returned was to avoid running into Cooper and Rory or any of their family. I'd always known that if I saw them, I would never have the strength to stay away and there was no way I could have kept Lily a secret. If I'd shown up with a baby in tow, word would have spread so quickly I would've gotten whiplash. So I'd stayed away. But now...now there were no more secrets. No reason to avoid Rory and Cooper or anyone else.

Which meant I could go to Bridgewater again. A bittersweet joy filled me at the thought of seeing Grandma's house—the house I'd grown up in. Was the tire swing still there or had the new owners taken it down? And my friends...I wondered if any of them were still in town. I was sure one or two still were.

Apparently, my feelings were clearly etched across my face because Aunt Sarah patted my arm. "I'm glad we got that settled."

————

COOPER

. . .

Once Ivy told us she was open to the idea of visiting Bridgewater again and showing Lily where she came from, Rory and I acted quickly. We booked tickets for all four of us a little later that week, giving Ivy just enough time to make the arrangements on her end and not too much time where she might change her mind. Since school was out for her and Lily, this just meant calling Lily's summer camp and telling them she'd be taking a vacation. Ivy had a job in Seattle and we knew this was just a visit, but it was a step in the right direction.

We showed up the morning of our flights and found a visibly excited Ivy with a giddy Lily waiting on the porch alongside their luggage. Aunt Sarah had been happy to wave us off on our adventure; I knew she was our secret champion as she wanted to see her niece happy and I was glad to know she thought that was with us.

Our daughter's eagerness for her first plane flight was infectious and Rory and I took turns sitting beside her on the plane and pointed out the window how small everything was below us. After the short flight to Bozeman and the drive to Bridgewater in the pickup truck we had left in the long-term lot, we took them to the house we'd bought in town and got them settled in. Even after a morning of travel, they were too excited to stay inside and Rory and I were more than happy to play tour guide. I was acting like a whipped man who was in love with the mother of his child...and said child.

For the first time in fuck knew, I felt good. Damn good. Hopeful.

I slept better, didn't think of my scars in the same way anymore. Lily had done that. With one quick share of her own "booboo," I'd been...better.

First stop, the western clothing store for a pair of pink

cowgirl boots for Lily. She wore them out of the store, her little sneakers tucked into Ivy's purse. The way she was strutting about in the new boots, I wasn't so sure we'd get them off her when she went to sleep.

As we walked down Main Street, Ivy couldn't seem to go more than a block in any direction without someone stopping her, greeting her with a hug and friendly questions about what she'd been up to these past seven years. No doubt news of her return—and of Lily's existence—would spread across town faster than a wildfire in high wind.

That was why, the next morning when we had breakfast at Jessie's diner, Ivy was more popular than ever. Jessie nearly dropped her tray when we walked in the door, and when she spotted Lily snuggled up against Ivy's side, I seriously thought she might faint.

She didn't, of course. I didn't think Jessie was the type to swoon, but it was damn close. It was probably the gossip that preceded us that prevented it. Instead, she came rushing over and ushered us to an empty booth like we were visiting royalty. Before we'd even settled into our seats, she started quizzing Ivy. Lily seemed to have gotten the hang of all these impromptu Q&A's her mama was subjected to and she chimed in right away that she was Ivy's daughter...and ours.

I wasn't sure I'd ever seen Jessie's eyes go so wide, even though she'd probably heard about it before now. Hearing it from Lily herself was something else entirely. She recovered quickly. "Well, of course you are, sweetheart. You clearly got the best traits from all of them."

Lily beamed up at her at that one. "I even have cowgirl boots!"

Jessie was a pro at fawning over the new boots—which Lily had worn to bed with her pink nightgown.

"What else have you been up to?" Jessie asked Ivy when Lily tucked her feet back beneath the booth. "You still in Seattle?"

Ivy nodded. "Yes, ma'am. Still living with my Aunt Sarah. I'm teaching second-grade."

Another table called out to Jessie and she gave them a nod. "I'll be right back," she said. "I want to hear all about it."

Of course, she did.

After she walked away, Rory turned to Ivy. "I can't believe you managed to raise a kid and get your degree in education." He shook his head in disbelief. "And all on your own."

I knew that still bothered him. He'd gotten over the fact that she'd decided not to tell us about Lily but I figured a little part of him still felt guilty that he hadn't been there. Like he'd let her and Lily down being on her own, even though there was no way he could have known.

She shrugged, thanking the other waitress who stopped by with mugs and poured the three of us coffee. "I wasn't alone, not entirely. I had Aunt Sarah. Grandma left me the house in her will and the sale of that covered tuition and most of our expenses until I could get a teaching job."

That must have been reassuring for her, the nest egg, even if it had come her way because of her grandmother's death.

I tensed, waiting for him to make another comment about how she could have reached out to us, but he surprised me. He reached across the table and took her hand. "I'm proud of you." He angled his head toward me. "We both are. You raised an amazing little girl—" He winked at Lily. "—and got the career of your dreams. Plus, you did it largely on your own."

I waggled my eyebrows at Lily who had taken the small jelly packets from the holder and began stacking them. "Your mama is pretty amazing, you know that?"

She nodded earnestly, an orange marmalade packet in her small hand. "I know."

Jessie returned to our table and she was wearing a smug smile along with her green uniform. "You're a second-grade teacher, right?" Jessie was not exactly subtle. She was up to something and it soon became clear what. "You know there's an opening at the Bridgewater Elementary School, don't you?"

I couldn't help but laugh. She'd helped us find Ivy and now she was helping us keep her.

Ivy shot us an amused look. She'd been gone for a while but she no doubt remembered Jessie's busybody ways. "No, I hadn't heard that."

"It's true." Jessie said goodbye to a couple as they walked toward the door. "Rocky Ashford gave his notice this past winter. He's retiring to Arizona so they're looking to hire his replacement."

"Mr. Ashford was my third-grade teacher," she said, then glanced at me and Rory. "Yours, too."

"Everyone in town since 1977," Jessie replied. "That spot's open come September."

A teaching job in Bridgewater. Two men. A new life. Ivy looked a little flustered, and I couldn't blame her. We'd promised we wouldn't try to pressure her and Lily to stay in Bridgewater. We'd go wherever they needed us and we meant it. I wanted them wherever I could have them. But Jessie seemed to have an agenda of her own. We might not have been the ones putting pressure on her, but she was surely feeling it.

A woman at the next booth came to Ivy's rescue when

she waved Jessie over. Fortunately, I didn't have to pipe up and tell Jessie to back off. It wouldn't be polite, but I'd do it if Ivy was getting upset.

I got a glimpse of the teenager beside the woman, and took notice of the ten or more holes lining up the side of her ear, the one in her eyebrow and corner of her lip. She had more holes in her than Swiss cheese. I glanced at Lily, busy once again with her jam tower. It wouldn't be long before she, too, wanted to bedazzle her body like that. Would I care?

Fuck, I was just getting used to a six-year-old. I could deal with teenage shit when the time came.

"Jessie, don't tell me you're adding headhunter to your list of careers alongside diner owner and matchmaker," the woman teased as she turned in her seat so she was facing us. The teenager rolled her eyes, obviously well aware, even at her age, that the diner owner was a meddler.

"I found you a job, didn't I?" Jessie gave a grudging grin. "Have y'all met Hannah yet? She's the new doctor in town, now that Dr. Roberts retired."

We all said our hellos to Hannah.

"This is Callie, my summer receptionist and these are my men, Cole and Declan." Hannah made the introductions.

We knew Cole and Declan, both a few years older than us, but Callie was new to us. She would have been close to Lily's age when we left for the army so that was no surprise.

"Ivy, welcome back to town," Cole said. Yes, he'd have remembered her as well.

"Are you here to stay?" Declan asked. While he was the head of police, he didn't wear a uniform, but I'd spotted his county-issued SUV when we pulled in the lot.

Ivy glanced in our direction before answering. I saw the uncertainty in her eyes. "I'm not sure yet."

Yet again, Hannah stepped in with the save. "Don't mind my nosy men, Ivy. They think anyone who leaves this town is crazy."

Ivy grinned. "I can understand why. It's a great place to live."

"It is, isn't it?" Hannah's smile was wide and friendly and it was clear that she and Ivy had taken a liking to each other.

Hannah turned her smile to include Jessie. "I might never have stayed here if it wasn't for this wonderful woman. She gave me my first job in town, and then introduced me to the old doctor so I could take over his practice."

Jessie was blushing—something I never thought I'd see.

"Don't forget the best part," Declan said.

Hannah laughed and rolled her eyes. It was obvious she was in love with her men. The happiness, the light in her eyes when she looked at either Dec or Cole made it obvious. "Oh yeah. She also nagged the heck out of me until I finally agreed to a date with these two." The two in question gave her smug grins and she leaned over to give them both a peck on the cheek.

Rory shot me a look and I knew what he was thinking. That right there—that was exactly what we wanted. An open relationship with our woman. To be able to kiss her and love her in public, like any other loving couple. We weren't afraid to show our love openly for Ivy, but if we lived in Seattle, we'd have to be careful about it. It wasn't just the three of us we had to worry about, but Lily. Little kids could be little shits. And their parents could be worse. Here, in Bridgewater, everyone was comfortable with a ménage relationship. Even kids. It was an everyday thing, seeing two husbands showing affection for their bride. No matter where we lived, no matter what Ivy ultimately wanted, we'd make it work.

But Ivy had just arrived back in Bridgewater and was still warming up to the idea of having Lily's fathers back in the picture. Hell, she hadn't been to town since her grandmother's funeral. Much as I wanted Ivy to embrace the idea of being our woman, we had to let her get there on her own. Seattle, Bridgewater, Bermuda. We didn't care. We'd show her how good it could be, but the rest was up to her. Even with some town meddling.

"And who's this?" Cole asked, his gaze fixed on Lily who was grinning up at them.

"This is my little girl—" Ivy hesitated then looked over at me and Rory. Blushed. "*Our* little girl, Lily."

I caught the look of surprise on Cole and Declan's faces —clearly the news hadn't reached them yet. With Jessie having official confirmation, the rest of the town should be well aware of our new father status by dinnertime.

"What do you think of Montana so far, Lily?" Jessie asked.

"I love it." Her childish enthusiasm had everyone smiling.

"What do you like best?" Declan asked. He had a sister, Cara, but as far as I knew, she didn't have a child with her husbands. No kids in that family yet.

"The animals. Rory said there were horses. Cows. Even moose." Her response was so quick, Rory, Ivy, and I shared a laugh. Our daughter had spent the entire plane ride asking questions about what animals she'd see on the ranches in Bridgewater and she'd been waiting not-so-patiently for us to show her some.

"I don't have any moose, but I have horses and cows at

my ranch," Cole said. "You're welcome to come out and see them."

Lily squealed with happiness, then hopped out of the booth and pranced like a horse around in a circle. "Can we? Can we?"

I looked to Ivy, who was smiling at Lily's exuberance. When a man wanted to pass, she hooked an arm around the little filly and pulled her out of the aisle.

"Are you guys up for it?" I asked, knowing if Lily had her way we wouldn't even wait until we had our breakfast.

Ivy nodded toward Lily. "Are you kidding? It would be a dream come true for this one. Let's do it."

Rory grimaced. "Sorry, but I'm going to have to skip this trip." Turning to me he added, "I've got to meet with the parts supplier over in Bozeman this afternoon. I already put him off last week while we were in Seattle."

I nodded, remembering we'd postponed the meeting. "I can take them to Cole's ranch and we'll meet up with you for dinner."

He looked to Ivy, then nodded. Running a finger down Lily's nose, he added, "I'll join you next time, squirt."

Lily didn't seem to care that Rory wouldn't be joining us. I imagined she wouldn't know who was with her when she got in front of the horses.

10

OOPER

Lily grew more and more excited the closer we got to Cole's ranch. Ivy and I laughed as she pointed out cows and deer she saw through the window like they were exhibits at the zoo.

"You know if you move here, she's going to have to get used to these sights," I said.

I looked over to see her biting her lip and mentally cursed myself for pushing the issue. Reaching over, I grabbed her hand, set it on my thigh so our fingers were joined. "*If* you move here," I added. "No pressure, remember? We could always come to you."

She gave me a smile as she squeezed my fingers. "Thanks for giving me room to decide. I appreciate it."

While her response was nice enough, it just opened the door for more questions. Was it just the location she was undecided on or was it a life with me and Rory? Did Bridgewater hold too many sad memories? Did she miss Seattle? I knew she enjoyed the hell out of fucking us, but she hadn't made a peep about her feelings. I could understand that she was more focused on Lily getting used to having fathers at the moment. To me, Lily was already used to having us in her life; kids were resilient like that. As for Ivy? She seemed to be the hold up. At some point, she was going to have to decide what she wanted for herself as well. And that included us.

When we pulled into the ranch, Cole and Hannah were waiting for us. There was no police SUV, and Cole said Declan had been on call and had to stay in town, but would catch up with us when his shift was over.

Cole led us toward the stables, although once we drew near Lily raced on ahead, her blond hair pulled back in a long tail, just like a pony's. By the time we joined her, she was standing in front of one of the stalls looking up at a white mare with unconditional love.

"That's Casper," Cole said to Lily. After a minute, he turned to us. "I think your daughter has Montana in her blood."

It sure as hell didn't come from me. While I knew which end of the animal was which, I'd only ridden a few times. Horses weren't for me and if I sat on one, I'd give cowboys a bad name.

"I think you're right." Ivy was smiling at her daughter but I saw the thoughtful look in her eye. "She's going to want one now."

I tried not to get my hopes up. I had no problem getting a horse for Lily. Hell, I'd hook the moon for her. There were many stables willing to board a horse, perhaps even Cole himself. It didn't matter where we were, just that we were together. Although, it would be a little weird to see a horse in Aunt Sarah's back yard.

"Can I ride her?" Lily asked, holding her hand up so the horse could sniff it.

"If it's all right with your mom and dad," Hannah replied.

Cole looked to us and I realized suddenly that *I* was the "dad" in the "mom and dad." I took a moment to savor it.

"She's as gentle as they come," Cole promised.

"It's all right with me," I said, but I looked to Ivy for final say. She'd made the decisions for Lily for six years and I didn't want to step on her toes now. She could have allergies or a fear of heights or something I knew nothing about.

Ivy nodded. "Me, too."

Cole got her situated on the horse, adjusting the stirrups to her size, settling her hands on the pommel. Ivy, Hannah, and I watched from the fence line as Cole led Lily and the horse. He was just going to walk them around the property a bit to give Lily a feel for the animal. I was already thinking ahead to how we could set her up with proper riding lessons if they moved here. It would be easier—and cheaper—than getting her that pony.

Then it happened. It was as if time stood still. I had no idea what caused the horse to rear up—snake, prairie dog or something else—and Cole was quick to rein Casper in, but not before Lily lost her balance and tumbled off. Her pink cowgirl boot got caught in the stirrup and she whacked her head on the ground.

Holy fuck. Casper was gentle?

"Lily!" Ivy screamed as we ran to her side. She was lying there, not moving, blood trickling from her forehead. Cole was holding onto the horse's lead, trying to keep her calm while trying to help Lily at the same time.

Panic had my heart racing and the terror I fought to keep at bay every day threatened to take control as I unhooked her foot from the stirrup. She was breathing but she wouldn't wake up even though Ivy kept shouting her name over and over.

Doctor. We needed a doctor! Fuck, we were out in the goddamn boonies. The moment I thought it, I was firmly pushed aside as Hannah knelt beside Lily. "Let me see her."

Hannah did a quick examination, her hands moving over Lily deftly and confidently, before looking up at us. Her grim expression did nothing to ease my panic.

I just found out I had a daughter. I couldn't lose her now.

Ivy gripped my hand and that brought the world back into focus. Ivy needed me. Lily needed me. I had to be strong for them.

Hannah was talking and I forced myself to pay attention to her words despite the roaring in my ears as my pulse rate rocketed.

"We need to get her to the hospital," she was saying. "I need access to their equipment to make sure she's all right. She hit her head and we need to make sure there's no swelling, no trauma we can't see. My clinic won't do."

Hospital. Yes. We needed to get to a hospital. Good. She had a plan to get my daughter help.

"The nearest one's in Bozeman," I said. "That's two hours away!"

"You can take her by helicopter. I'll be with her. With both of you," Hannah promised.

I nodded. "Yes. Good idea. Rory can fly her."

"Rory's not here. Oh my god, he's *in* Bozeman for that meeting." I never wanted to hear the panic in Ivy's voice ever again. Her desperate eyes turned to me. "You'll fly her."

I stared at Ivy as if she told me I was to fly us to the moon in a rocket, not to Bozeman in a helicopter.

"No." The one word escaped my lips and I looked away. I wanted to throw up. God, no.

Hannah's hands were on my shoulders, her grip firm, forcing me to face her. She looked fiercer than my commanding officer in the army. "Listen to me, Cooper. You're licensed. Experienced. You have the chopper. I need you to fly us."

I looked from her to Ivy, but Ivy was solely focused on Lily. The fear in her expression was heartbreaking to see.

I shook my head. "I can't." *I can't.* The words were there. I didn't say them but Hannah must have seen my hesitation because her grim expression intensified. "I can't pilot one again." When she frowned, I admitted my worst. "I killed six of my men. The chopper was hit and we went down. They... they all died."

I remembered the heat, the warning bells that filled the chopper's cabin. The smoke. One of the men screaming in pain. The way the desert got bigger and bigger as I fought for control. Waking up, a section of the chopper embedded in my arm and shoulder. Silence. I was sweating, but cold all at the same time.

Compassion softened Hannah's gaze, but not her resolve. "We're not at war. No one will be shooting at us. Lily needs care *now* and you're her best bet."

Cole tugged me to my feet, put his hands on my shoulders. His gaze was serious. "We need you to do this, Cooper. Ivy needs you. Your daughter needs you."

Your daughter needs you. They were quite possibly the only words that could have broken through that terror-induced haze. Lily needed me.

I nodded and Cole scooped Lily up into his arms, her

body wilted and completely void of all her exuberance and boundless energy.

Yes, Lily needed me to be strong. I hadn't saved my men, but I could save her. Reaching down, I helped Ivy to stand. "Come on," I said, nudging her toward Cole's truck, which was the closest. I could do this. I could save my daughter. "We've got to get Lily to the hospital."

11

My heart was racing as I sped to the Bozeman hospital. Cole had called me several times, but I'd had my phone on silent during my meeting, only to hear his frantic messages when it was over. Dread had my stomach churning. This was just like before. The same overwhelming cascade of emotions I'd had when I'd gotten the call that Cooper had been in an accident. That he was in the combat hospital being stabilized and readied for transport to Germany. Knowing his chopper had gone down, but not what his injuries were.

This sense of helplessness was sickening. Someone I loved was hurt and there was nothing I could do. If something happened to Lily...if she didn't make it.

I cut off that line of thought before this anxiety turned into outright panic. Thinking of the worst possible scenario wouldn't do anybody any good. But still, the ache in my gut refused to go away. The pain in my heart was excruciating. I couldn't go through this again. Never again.

Fuck! I slapped my hand on the wheel and tried to catch my breath. I slammed on my brakes and parked in the fire lane, not caring if my car got towed.

I found Cooper and Ivy in the ER waiting room talking to Hannah. Ivy sobbed when she saw me and came running into my arms. I shot Cooper a terrified look.

"Lily's okay," he said, his voice steady, but full of emotion. "She's got a concussion, no internal bleeding. She's going to be fine."

My knees practically buckled in relief. I was supposed to be the strong one, to take care of Ivy, but I felt as if she were the one holding me up, comforting me.

Cooper looked pale but happier than I'd seen him in months. I held Ivy closer and stroked her back as she cried in relief. A little while later a nurse came out to find us. She looked between the three of us. "Who are Lily's parents?"

Ivy spoke first. "We all are."

We all are. Cooper gave me a small smile over her head, but I was too focused on seeing Lily to think about anything else. My anxiety still hadn't eased and I knew it wouldn't until I saw her for myself.

She was asleep in her room when we arrived, but her cheeks were flushed and aside from an IV in her arm and a white bandage on her forehead, she looked whole enough. I took her tiny hand in mine and only then did I let myself revel in the realization that she really was okay. She was going to be just fine and she would be in our lives every day —no matter what. I didn't care where. It didn't matter.

When she opened her eyes and smiled up at us, I was sure my heart was going to burst out of my chest. I'd had no idea I could love anyone so much, or in such a short amount of time. It was different than the way I loved Ivy. I loved her unconditionally, but this...this intensity I felt for Lily, well, it was pure.

It wiped away the painful memories and all thoughts of *what ifs*. I'd led Cooper to boot camp. I'd led him to war and he'd paid a hefty price, a price that still haunted him and would the rest of his life. His family almost lost him. Me? I'd had no family like him, nothing to come home to. Until now.

I had Cooper, sure, but now we were a family. Not just with Ivy, but with Lily, too. The past led us all to this moment. There would always be risks in this life—the more I loved, the more I risked losing. But looking at Lily, and turning to see the smiling faces of Ivy and Cooper—I knew it would be worth it.

This, right here in this room, was the family I'd never had but always wanted.

After a short visit, Lily started to yawn and the nurse told us she'd be tired from the medicine. Hannah had already told us they'd keep her overnight for observation because of the concussion, but everyone expected her to make a full recovery.

I called a local hotel and made a reservation while Ivy explained to Lily that we'd be staying the night. "One of us will always be here with you throughout the night," she explained, sitting on the edge of her bed. "You have nothing to worry about." She stroked her daughter's hair and gave her the best smile she could manage considering her eyes were puffy from crying and the stress of the day had taken its toll.

The stress had taken a toll on all of us. Holy hell, I never wanted to go through that again.

It was only around dinnertime, but we all looked and

felt exhausted. Hannah came in then to check on her patient. After checking a few vitals, she turned to the three of us. "She's doing great." Sizing us up, she gave us a sympathetic smile. "You three, on the other hand...."

Turning back to our daughter, she said, "Lily, what do you say if I take the first shift so your parents can go get cleaned up and maybe even rest a bit?"

"Can we watch TV?" Lily asked, her eyes lighting up at the prospect of a TV in her own room.

Hannah grinned at us over her shoulder. "We absolutely can."

With that decided, she shooed the three of us out the door. "Go get some food and rest," she ordered. "Lily and I will be just fine."

Ivy hesitated in the doorway. "Are you sure? I should stay, in case she gets upset."

Hannah's look was firm but gentle as she placed her hands-on Ivy's shoulders and steered her toward the hallway. "She's going to be just fine. Take a minute to breathe. To unwind before you blow your top. I'll be with her the whole time."

Ivy still looked doubtful. "Cole and Declan are picking me up and they won't get into town for another couple of hours, at least. Go."

When Cooper and I hesitated once more, she rolled her eyes. "For heaven's sake, you three, I'm her doctor and we're in the hospital. No horsing around allowed."

That got a smile from Ivy, but I doubted Lily would be allowed near a horse ever again.

"She's in good hands, I promise."

"Can I wear my cowgirl boots with my hospital outfit?" Lily asked.

I couldn't help but laugh at that. Yeah, she was fine. With

that reassurance and Hannah pulling the little boots out of a bag with the rest of Lily's clothes, the three of us headed out.

After we checked in to the hotel, Cooper and Ivy filled me in on what had happened. All Cole had told me on the phone was that Lily fell off a horse. I wrapped a supportive arm around Ivy as she choked up at the memory of seeing Lily fall off, hit her head and lay there unconscious on the ground.

I was freaking out at just the thought of it. Being there must have been horrible.

When they got to the part where Cooper flew them from Bridgewater to the hospital, I stared at my best friend in openmouthed shock. I'd been too heartsick and worried to think about how they'd gotten to the hospital so quickly. I'd just been grateful that they'd gotten there and hadn't worried about how. Now, though, I stared at Cooper in stunned admiration.

He'd said he'd never fly again. We'd run a chopper company, but he'd ride a desk. I'd take all the flights, or we'd hire someone to help. I had no intention of pushing him on it. I hadn't crashed in the middle of the desert. I hadn't been under enemy fire. I hadn't lost all the men looking to me to get them out of danger.

He'd come through, barely, despite the demons he battled. He'd somehow gotten behind the stick and saved our girl. When our woman and our daughter were in trouble, he'd stepped up, like I always knew he could. "You did what?"

He ducked his head with a bashful grin. His cheeks flushed a ruddy red. "I flew. Fuck, I was so scared." I wasn't sure if he was referring to piloting a chopper again or because Lily had been hurt.

I looked over to Ivy and saw her giving Cooper a proud

smile. "He did it for us. For Lily." She reached over and took his hand in hers. Squeezed until her knuckles turned white. "We needed him and he was there for us."

I reached over to put a hand on his shoulder. "I'm proud of you, man."

His expression was beyond embarrassed at the recognition, but he was clearly pleased. "You know, I don't think I could have gotten back in the cockpit for any other reason. And while I wish the accident had never happened, fuck, I never want to see Lily hurt ever again, I'm glad it forced me to face my fears." He turned to me, his expression resolute. "I think you and I should split piloting duties at our company. And the damn paperwork."

I grinned like an idiot. For the first time in a long while, I saw my old friend again, or at least a hint of him. It wasn't a full recovery, but it was a start. "I think that sounds like a great plan."

He looked down at his feet and then back up at Ivy. "Wherever we are. Seattle, Bridgewater, we can run our business."

Ivy didn't say anything to that. Now wasn't the time to get her to decide, but I knew Cooper wanted to ensure she knew we would go where she was. Where our daughter was.

"If it's all right with you, I'd like to take the first shift with Lily tonight," he added.

Ivy smiled, cupped his cheek. "Of course. And she's your daughter, too. You don't need to ask my permission to spend time with her."

His grin was easygoing, boyish—the old smile I hadn't seen in nearly a year. "In that case, I'd better take a quick shower and get out of here."

When he shut the bathroom door behind him, the water kicking on, Ivy leaned against me, her head on my shoulder.

"That was a great thing you did for Cooper," I said. "Helping him face his fears. He needed that."

"It was unintentional, I assure you. I wish there had been a different way to get him to fly." I felt her shudder, probably thinking about what happened. "I didn't do anything, really, it was just the circumstance."

I shook my head. "No, that's not all it was. I'm not really talking about the accident either." She turned to look up at me, a frown on her face. Clearly, she didn't understand, so I continued. "He needed someone to care about again. Someone to care for. You and Lily are exactly what he needs in his life to help him move on. He knows I'm here for him. He knows his parents are—you'll meet them soon—but it's not the same. You're...more."

She smiled. "Then I'm glad we could be that for him." She paused for a moment. "But what are we to you, Rory?"

I grinned down at her. "Do you even need to ask? You, Lily, and Cooper are everything to me. I love you all so much. You're my family."

I saw a glimmer of tears in her eyes at that, but she blinked them back.

Reaching out, I cupped her chin in my hand so she was forced to look up at me. "We need you, Ivy. We always have. I hope you can see that now."

She gave me a wobbly smile, nodded. "What I see is that Lily and I need you and Cooper just as much as you need us."

Cooper appeared in the doorway of the bathroom and I saw the intense emotions play across his face. I hadn't heard the water shut off, but he stood in just a towel about his waist, water beading on his chest, dripping from his hair.

I already knew the answer, but I asked him anyway. "Did you hear that?"

His answer was a growl. "About time she admitted as much."

Ivy's laugh was soft and beautiful. "Maybe it took me a little time to get used to the idea, but I get it now. The four of us are a family." She nudged me with her shoulder. "Always have been, always will be."

12

VY

Maybe it was the adrenaline from the accident that had me seeing so clearly. More likely it was being reminded of how easy it was to lose someone I loved. Lily had fallen so quickly. One second she was happily sitting upon Casper plodding along, the next, dangling by her shiny new cowgirl boot.

It had been horrifying and I never wanted to feel that level of panic ever again. She'd woken in the helicopter and because of that, Hannah became optimistic, but I hadn't truly calmed down until the ER doc ruled out everything but a concussion. I was still shaking and I knew exactly what I wanted to do.

No more debating. No more worries. We just had to live and hope—pray—for the best. The decision to be with these men, really be with them, suddenly felt like a no brainer. We'd wasted enough time apart these past seven years. The last thing I wanted was to waste any more. Perhaps I'd known the inevitable when they stood outside my school, all sexy brawn and brooding stares, but now I was certain.

The way they were looking at me right now—the brooding was hidden by the obvious love, their love—I'd never felt more certain and I told them as much.

"I love you," Cooper said. "I've always loved you, sweets."

Rory nodded. "We claimed you, body and heart, all those years ago."

I swallowed back tears that threatened. We'd been through so much today, I was done with tears, even if they were happy ones.

"Well, all right then," Rory said with a grin. A grin that could make my panties wet. "I guess now we just need to figure out how to relocate our business to Seattle."

His words had the smile slip from my face. Oh god. These men. Tears filled my eyes. They had assumed all along that to be with me and Lily they'd have to move away from Bridgewater. They were willing to give up the town and family nearby. A business. A home they owned. Everything just because I said I wanted to stay in Seattle. I was humbled by them, by the depth of their desire to be with us.

I shook my head. "Don't do that. Not yet, at least."

From the moment I'd stepped off the plane and breathed in the clear Montana air, I'd felt at home in a way I hadn't for ages. Being back in Bridgewater felt right. It had been nice to see my childhood home and the school I'd gone to, but that wasn't what had made me think that Lily and I might be better off moving back. It had been the people. Their friendliness and openness. The way threesomes like Hannah and her men went about their lives with no hassles or strange looks.

That's what I'd grown up with and that was what I wanted for Lily. I wanted her to be close with both her daddies and not have to hide the fact that she had two fathers. And I didn't want to hide either. I loved these men—both of them. The three of us fit. We belonged together. And I wanted to share that with everyone, not hide it away like a dirty secret.

Cooper and Rory were watching me, waiting for me to explain.

"I think—" I started. I bit my lip as I felt the full heat of their stares. "I think maybe we should stay here in Montana. Lily seems to like it here and I've missed my home."

Rory and Cooper were outright grinning at me.

"Are you sure?" Cooper asked.

I nodded. Yeah, this was right. It felt right. "I just need to talk to Aunt Sarah first and see if she'd like to join us." There was a lot I had to sort out, like a job and Lily's new school, but I wouldn't be doing it alone. Now that I'd made my decision, all doubts and confusion lifted and for the first time in a long time, I knew I was on the right path. It might have taken me a while to sort it all out, but we were all here, together—healthy and whole—and that was what mattered.

I couldn't wait to tell Lily. Seeing her expression when she'd first taken in the majestic mountains and the untouched nature...I knew she would be over the moon. Turned out, my men had been right. She had Bridgewater in her blood, just like I did.

I turned to Cooper. "Will you wait for me to get ready? I'll go back to the hospital with you, I just want to freshen up."

Rory stood and pulled me to my feet. "Lily is still sleeping, there's no rush." He tugged me toward the bathroom, where Cooper was still standing in the doorway, a towel slung around his hips. I noticed he didn't try to hide his scars from me this time and for that I was glad.

I looked between the two, saw the heat in their eyes, their intention.

"It's like that, is it?" I asked, a smile forming.

"Fuck yeah," Cooper said.

"Let me...let me check in with Hannah first, okay?"

Rory stepped back, grabbed my phone, dialed. "Hannah? It's Rory. How's our little squirt? Yeah, good. Tell that to Ivy."

He passed me the phone and then stripped off his shirt. He was too relaxed for anything to be wrong.

"Hi, Hannah," I said, staring at Rory's rugged chest. I loved the smattering of dark hair and the way it ran into a line that disappeared beneath his jeans. I knew exactly where it led and I could see the thick outline of his cock.

I listened as Hannah told me Lily had had two chocolate puddings and a lime Jell-o before she fell asleep. She reassured me that I could take time with Rory and Cooper, that I wasn't being a bad mother taking a few hours for myself.

I handed the phone back to Rory.

"All good?" Cooper asked, coming over to me, stroking my hair back from my face. I told him about our daughter's little pig-out and he laughed. "That's my girl. Feel better?"

I nodded and didn't resist when he grabbed my t-shirt and pulled it over my head.

"Thanks for letting me check on her." I closed my eyes as his hands cupped my lace covered breasts.

"You don't have to thank us for making sure our daughter is okay. But now that she is..."

He didn't say more, only dropped to his knees and undid the front of my jeans. It took a little work, but he tugged the snug fabric down and off, then hooked the lacy edge of my panties to follow. Cooper unhooked my bra and slipped it off my shoulders so I was bare to them.

I couldn't have said no if I'd wanted to. The feel of Cooper's lips on my neck made my knees go weak and I leaned back against him. After such a stressful day, I turned to putty in their arms. I let myself revel in the fact that I had two caring, sexy, kind men to take care of me. Two men who wanted nothing more than to make me happy.

"Why don't you let us help you relax." Rory looked at me with his dark eyes, all heated with simmering need just before he leaned in and kissed the top of my pussy. My hand lowered to his short hair, too short to tangle, but silky beneath my palm.

"Okay. Oh! Yes," I breathed.

Rory knew exactly how to touch me, to lick me, to nibble and suck on my clit to push me to the brink. When he slipped a finger inside me and curled, I stiffened. When Cooper tugged on my nipples and nipped at the spot where my shoulder met my neck, I came.

They continued to touch me as I came back to myself. I felt Cooper's lips on my neck, Rory's gentle kisses on my clit, their hands on me, caressing me. Gentling me.

I didn't even realize I was grinning until Rory stood then kissed the corner of my lips. "What are you smiling about?"

"I'm just happy," I said, tasting myself as his tongue met mine. "After everything the three of us have been through, I never would have thought we'd get our fairytale ending, but now...."

"I'm not sure how many fairy tales have the princess eaten out by one of her princes while the other other plays with her nipples."

I rolled my eyes, but had to laugh. "That is so dirty."

"Then let's get you clean," Cooper said, stepping back and tugging me to the bathroom, dropping the towel from his waist on the way.

I looked over my shoulder and watched as Rory stripped, then joined us.

Cooper moved away from me and Rory wrapped his arms around my waist, holding me up. I heard the shower start behind me and my men helped me in. The feel of the hot water against my overly sensitive skin made me gasp, then moan as Rory and Cooper joined me, their hard chests now hot and slick as they pressed against me from both sides. They caressed my breasts, my ass, my pussy, using soap to make me slick, then rinsed me and did it all over again. Soon I was wiggling between them, writhing at the delicious torture.

I let my head fall back on Cooper's shoulder as Rory lowered himself to suck on my nipples. Moving back and forth, he used his teeth to nip and tease the tender flesh until I was whimpering, Cooper's strong grip on my hips the only thing keeping me from shamelessly rubbing my pussy against Rory's thigh so I could find my release. Again. They'd turned me into a desperate hussy and I didn't care.

I was so needy for them, begging for more when Cooper teased me by slipping one finger between my folds, stroking my clit before sliding into my pussy. My hips jerked and I heard Rory's low laugh. "I think our woman is ready for us, what do you think?"

Cooper reached around me to tweak one nipple. "I think we should give her what she needs."

Yes! Oh holy hell, yes.

"I *need* you in me. Stop playing and give it to me."

My voice was bossy and Rory chuckled.

"Yes, ma'am."

They took turns *giving it to me*. Just like that memorable night out in Baker's field all those years ago, my men took turns fucking me. One would fuck me shamelessly as the other held me upright and whispered words of love in my ear. Rory took me from behind, Cooper as I was pressed up against the tile, my legs wrapped around his waist. I came three times before it was all over, and by that time they had to help me dry off and carry me out to the bed since my legs refused to work. My brain was mush and I was okay with that. I knew my men would take care of me.

"I love knowing we wore you out. You need a nap, sweets," Cooper whispered as he tucked me in and then climbed in beside me.

Rory lay down on my other side so I was cocooned between them, just where I wanted to be. Between them. Always.

"Sleep, then we'll head over to the hospital and see our daughter."

Yes, our daughter. I loved the pride I heard in Cooper's voice. "We're a family now," Rory murmured.

Yes. A family. I found myself smiling as I drifted off. We'd join Lily, stay with her until we could take her home in the morning, then go home to Bridgewater. All of us. Our whole family. Together.

WANT MORE?

———

Read the first chapter of Hold Me Close, book 4 in the Bridgewater County Series!

———

HOLD ME CLOSE - EXCERPT

RACHEL

Even though I was born and raised in Montana, I'd never really understood the appeal of the rodeo circuit. The animals, wrangling them, tying little calves' ankles up as fast as possible. But as I watched this cowboy riding the massive bull, the muscles of his chest rippling beneath the fabric of his shirt as his arms bulged beneath the strained material, I finally got it. He rocked back and forth, balancing and going with the jerky motions of the angry beast, arm flung up over his head.

Oh Lordy, I got it.

I gasped when the bull kicked out its hind legs, not because I was scared for the cowboy but because of the way his thighs contracted beneath those jeans to stay on its back. Jeans, I might add, that left little to the imagination. The whole thing was stupid, plain stupid. Stay on a bull for eight seconds, but somehow every one of my hot buttons was pushed watching the testosterone-fest.

"Here's a napkin." My sister's voice cut into my

openmouthed gawking. I turned to face Emmy, who somehow still managed to look sleek and stylish in a jean skirt and flowy top even when eight months pregnant. She held out one of the napkins she'd nabbed when she'd gone to get herself an ice cream cone.

I frowned at it. "What's that for?"

Emmy grinned. "You've got a little drool there."

My frown turned into a scowl. "I was not drooling." I turned away and subtly swiped the corners of my mouth just in case.

"Whatever you say, sis." I didn't have to see her to know she was rolling her eyes in my direction. Even though she was younger, Emmy had the air of a know-it-all older sister. But then, she was the one who was happily married with a baby on the way while I was still deeply rooted in spinsterhood with no end in sight. Somehow, this seemed to give her an advantage that negated my two years' seniority.

Emmy had a Bridgewater marriage, which meant she was the lucky bride of two doting, protective men. Like all my siblings, she had a big heart and a good head on her shoulders and I wished only the best for her. Except for now. As she licked her ice cream, looking impossibly smug, I wondered for the millionth time how my bratty little sister managed to snag not one, but two men, when I hadn't managed to land a second date in more months than I'd cared to admit.

It was fine and all if it were just Emmy having a baby, but I was one of six. All five of my siblings were married with kids, or in Emmy's case, with a kid on the way. Two of my brothers were in Bridgewater marriages as well, but the rest had followed in my parents' footsteps and gone the traditional route. One man, one woman. And everyone had found their "perfect someone" or "perfect someones" early.

Emmy was only twenty-four and my brother, Zach, had married at twenty-one. My parents always used to say, "When you know, you know."

Well, I'd yet *to know.*

Honest to God, I didn't care what kind of relationship I found myself in—traditional, Bridgewater, or other—I just wanted to be in one. Not that I was desperate for a man. No, I didn't sit around the house pining for one. Besides, I didn't just want *any* man, I wanted the right man...or men. I dated, but so far there hadn't been any spark, not anyone that I'd wanted to go out with past a second date. So I'd sort of given up. Not that I'd ever been on the prowl, but I wasn't going to bars with my girlfriends on Friday nights looking for hook-ups. Well, I'd never gone looking for a hook-up, but I'd gone looking. And it hadn't worked.

Because of this, I wasn't exactly boy crazy, but I definitely was baby crazy. I wasn't old, by any means, but I'd thought that by twenty-six I'd be in the same boat as the rest of my family. If not married with kids, at least well on my way. Heck, Emmy was having a baby before me. Yeah, that hurt, not that I'd ever tell her or let it show. It was my problem, not hers. It wasn't her fault she found two guys who loved her and wanted to make a life with her. A family.

I'd had it all planned out. College, grad school, then start a family. Sure, I was young, but I wanted a big brood and that meant starting early. But somehow, at some point, my life plan had gotten derailed. I stifled a sigh as I turned to watch the hottie cowboy pick up his hat from the dirt ring, lift it and wave it in air. The crowd cheered and clapped as he walked out through the open rail. Even the back of him looked damn good in the chaps and snug jeans. They were well worn and molded his butt *just* right.

Dammit. Emmy nudged me with her hip, caught me

ogling again. "You should go back there. Introduce yourself."

I looked at her as if she had suggested I climb on the back of the bull and go for a ride. "Introduce myself? To the bull rider? I couldn't do that."

Emmy glanced at me. We looked similar with our light brown hair and hazel eyes but she was several inches shorter. "Why not?"

I shrugged. Because I *couldn't*. I wasn't like Emmy. She had no problem going up to strange men and flirting—well, she hadn't before she'd fallen for Rick and Kevin two years ago. They were alpha males through and through and they were the only men she flirted with now. The bowling ball beneath her shirt proved that.

But that wasn't me. I'd never been great at flirting and super attractive men tended to make me nervous. No, I always turned into a stuttering idiot. The reason behind my single status wasn't such a mystery after all.

"You're intimidated, aren't you?" Emmy continued. God, she was way too amused by my discomfort. Some things never changed.

"By that guy?" I pointed in the direction he'd gone. "Absolutely. You saw him. He's...insanely hot. Of course, I'm intimidated."

I didn't bother denying it. We both knew I was the reserved one in our family. That was the way I put it. Emmy and my other sisters just called me a prude. What they didn't know—what I'd never told them—was that my wariness around hot men, well, practically all men, wasn't just because they intimidated me. It went deeper than that. I knew that if they got close, they'd want to get *close*. I'd had exactly one attempt at sex and it had been awful. Scary.

Back in college, there'd been a guy. A good guy...or so I'd

thought. On our third date, he'd assumed we'd be doing more than just kissing. He'd assumed wrong. I hadn't been ready to take it to the next level, but he wouldn't listen. His hands had been everywhere despite my protests and my feeble attempts to push him off me. He'd been too strong, too determined.

I shivered under the June sun. Thank god, my roommate had come in when she had or who knows how far it would have gone. As it was, he'd groped and fondled but never managed to get my pants off. Still, the experience had left me with a bad taste in my mouth whenever dates started to get too close. I froze up. Panicked. My stomach still turned when I thought of how the jerk's hands had felt on my skin and no matter how attracted I was to a guy, that was all I could think of whenever a man leaned in for a kiss.

Needless to say, intimacy was not exactly my strong suit.

I didn't say any of that to Emmy, however. It wouldn't have made a difference. Her mouth was set in a stubborn line.

"Go on, say hello," she said. Her eyes were filled with a familiar mischievousness. The kind of look she used to give right before I walked into whatever booby-trap she'd laid for me in our shared bedroom.

"Why?" My eyes narrowed with suspicion. She wouldn't just push me to flirt with any old guy. "Do you know him or something?"

"Or something." She nodded, barely able to contain her laughter. "You will, too. He's your new boss."

I blinked at her uncomprehendingly for a moment, but then her words clicked and my brain registered their meaning.

"My boss?" That perfect specimen of man was my new boss? Emmy had been working as the office manager for a local guest ranch, Hawk's Landing, since she graduated college. She'd be leaving in a matter of weeks to have the baby and didn't plan to return to work. Since I'd just moved home after finishing up my master's degree in Denver, Emmy had talked her employers into giving me the job sight unseen.

It was a good job in my field and I'd been grateful for the opportunity. But now...I stared after the large, manly man who'd walked off toward the stables and I tried to still the butterflies in my belly. Well, now I was nervous for so many reasons.

I couldn't work for a man like that. How was I supposed to interact with a hottie cowboy and still maintain any sort of professionalism? I'd be a stammering, bumbling fool around him.

"He's not a professional bull rider?" The way he'd pivoted and rocked his hips on that bull made me wonder what he'd be like using them for riding something else, like me. Was the sun getting hotter?

"Nope. He does it just for fun."

Fun. Taunting every conscious female, more likely.

Emmy's voice was laced with laughter. "If you think he's gorgeous, wait until you meet his business partner."

I turned to see if she was serious. She was. Oh shit. "There are two of them?" My mind reeled. Two hot men would be my new employers. Oh, Lord help me.

She nodded and wrapped an arm around me as she steered me in the direction of the stables. "Go on," she urged. "You need to meet the owners eventually. You might as well introduce yourself to Matt now. Get it over with."

I looked over with apprehension. "Why, is he a jerk or something?"

Her head dropped back as she let out a loud laugh like

I'd just said something hilarious. "A jerk? Nah. Matt is sweet as can be. I just meant it'd be better for you to meet him now, somewhere casual, before he becomes your boss."

"I don't know," I hedged, dragging my feet as she attempted to lead me.

She came to a stop and I nearly toppled over. Dropping her arm from my waist, she placed her fists on her hips as she turned to face me with her know-it-all look that I hated. Mainly, because when she wore it, she was typically right. Like now. "Rachel Andrews, if you don't conquer your nerves about meeting this man you're going to be useless as his office manager."

I pressed my lips together, wishing she wasn't right. I needed to do this. I had to rip off the Band-Aid and get over my nerves. Nerves which were completely unfounded. She'd worked for Matt for years and I hadn't once heard of him being an asshole. No doubt her husbands would pound him into the ground if he so much as hurt Emmy's feelings, let alone something worse.

Fearless, that was me. Fine, I'd go meet my gorgeous, jaw-dropping boss.

I gave her a short nod before I could change my mind and headed toward the stables. Right, I could do this. I took a deep breath.

I can do this, I can do this. I chanted that line over and over until I entered the crowded stable, the powerful smell of hay and horses tickled my nose. There were a number of dusty, sweaty cowboys but just as many scantily-clad buckle bunnies who swarmed around like gnats.

Just like any other sport where there were powerful, attractive men, there were the women who were looking to bed them. I was way overdressed in comparison. I had on boots and jeans and a pale pink snap shirt. I wasn't frumpy, by any means, but I didn't let it all hang out at a dusty rodeo. Not like these women. Most wore camisoles or slinky tees and short shorts. One buxom blonde to my right was very clearly wearing no bra. It wasn't cold at all, but it was below freezing out if her pointy nipples were anything to go by.

I looked away, glanced around the milling people, trying to find my new boss. Since it was the county fair, there were more events going on than just the rodeo. I didn't see Matt, only met the curious gazes of other cowboys and the women who clung to them.

I tugged at the edge of my shirt and tucked my chin as I headed further into the breach. I felt ridiculously out of place. I wasn't the only woman with a buttoned-down shirt, but I was the only one who wasn't wearing it opened halfway down my chest to show off a lacy bra. I definitely did not belong, but I'd come this far. There was no way I could turn back now. Emmy would never let me live it down. I was just meeting my new boss. That was it. He wasn't a smokin' hot cowboy. *He was my boss.*

Boss. Boss. Boss.

Get Hold Me Close now!

GET A FREE BOOK!

JOIN MY MAILING LIST TO BE THE FIRST TO KNOW OF NEW
RELEASES, FREE BOOKS, SPECIAL PRICES AND OTHER
AUTHOR GIVEAWAYS.

http://freeromanceread.com

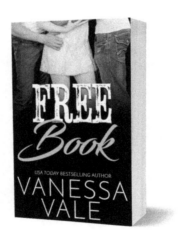

ABOUT THE AUTHOR

Vanessa Vale is the *USA Today* Bestselling author of over 50 books, sexy romance novels, including her popular Bridgewater historical romance series and hot contemporary romances featuring unapologetic bad boys who don't just fall in love, they fall hard. When she's not writing, Vanessa savors the insanity of raising two boys and figuring out how many meals she can make with a pressure cooker. While she's not as skilled at social media as her kids, she loves to interact with readers.

www.vanessavaleauthor.com

ALSO BY VANESSA VALE

Grade-A Beefcakes

Sir Loin Of Beef

T-Bone

Tri-Tip

Porterhouse

Skirt Steak

Small Town Romance

Montana Fire

Montana Ice

Montana Heat

Montana Wild

Montana Mine

Steele Ranch

Spurred

Wrangled

Tangled

Hitched

Lassoed

Bridgewater County Series

Ride Me Dirty

Claim Me Hard

Take Me Fast

Hold Me Close

Montana Men Series

The Lawman

The Cowboy

The Outlaw

Standalone Reads

Twice As Delicious

Western Widows

Sweet Justice

Mine To Take

Relentless

Sleepless Night

Man Candy - A Coloring Book